Mary Weeks Millard

The ACE
Survival Team

DayOne

Designed by **documen**
Printed by TJ International

Dedications

For Martha, Zoe and Joe, who understand all about homeschooling and international schools and life in a missionary family. Also for their friends Sam, Megan and Emily, who are now, back in school in England. May the Lord continue to bless and help each of you as you follow him.

This is dedicated to all the pilots in MAF and AIMAir and other such organisations who faithfully and bravely serve the Lord and their passengers.

Acknowledgments

My thanks to Joel Holm of MedAir who helped me research the Cessna planes.

My thanks to DayOne staff, especially Youth Director Tirzah Jones and Chris Jones for her editing.

My thanks to friends who have taken the time to read this book and comment on it.

My thanks as always to Malcolm my patient and supportive husband.

Chapter one

Luke sat on his bed watching his mum pack his suitcase. Inside he was bubbling over with excitement, but he was also scared. He had waited so long for this day to come, but now that it had arrived he hoped he would be ready for this big change in his life. For the first time, he was going to school!

Luke was ten years old and because his parents worked in an African country called Democratic Republic of Congo, up until now his mum had homeschooled him. That meant that she gave him lessons each day at home. He still had to take tests and do homework, but it was lonely in a classroom with only his mum as teacher, even though he had enjoyed the lessons. Tomorrow he was going by plane to Kenya to a big International School. There would be lots of children of his age to play with. He was longing to be in a football team!

"Nearly done Luke!" said his mother. "I'll leave your blazer on the chair ready for you to wear in the morning. I'm just going to bake some of your favourite cookies to add to your tuck box. Do you want to go round the village and say goodbye to your friends while I do the cooking?"

"Yes please, Mum," Luke answered and swung his legs off the bed. In two minutes he was out of the little bungalow and running down the dirt track to the village.

He whistled and Shenzi his dog appeared and followed him. Even Shenzi seemed to know that something different was happening. Luke ruffled his dog's ear and told him that he would be back in three months. Together they went to the next house and Luke called out. "Hodi?" which means "Can I come in?" A weak voice called out "Karibu" (You're welcome).

"Mama Beti, I've come to say goodbye. I'm going to proper school tomorrow and won't be home until Christmas. The plane is coming in the morning to take me to Kenya", explained Luke. "I expect you will hear it when it comes to the air strip."

"That is very exciting for you," answered the old lady. "I shall miss you coming in to talk to me Luke, but I'm sure you will love the school."

"I hope so," said Luke, "There will be lots of other children for me to play with and new lessons to learn."

"That's good," replied Mama Beti," but don't forget how to speak our language, I will want to hear about everything when you come home!"

Luke gave his neighbour a big hug, then went running out, with Shenzi at his heels, to the next house. He knew everyone in the small village and could speak the Kingwana language almost as well as his native English.

The last house he visited was where his special friend, Manweli lived. It was hard to say goodbye to him, even though he was really longing to go to school. Manweli was nine and the two boys spent a lot of time together, playing and having adventures. Going away to school was one adventure that his friend couldn't share.

"When I come home at Christmas, we'll make a dam in the river and go swimming," promised Luke, "It will be dry season by then and we'll have great fun. You will come to wave me off in the plane, won't you?" he asked Manweli.

"Of course I will. And I'll take Shenzi out for walks and let your goat stay with our flock. I shall ask your mother to help me make a chart and I can mark off the days until you come home. That will help me not to miss you too much!" replied Manweli.

Just before suppertime, Luke's father came home. He had been to the nearest town to get supplies.

"I've got a present for you," he said to Luke, handing him a small package. Excitedly Luke tore off the brown paper in which it was wrapped. Inside was a mobile phone! He was so excited!

"Thank you soooo much!" he said, giving his dad a hug. "Does this mean I can talk to you?"

"I have put a Kenyan sim card inside and although we have no signal here in the village, I should be able to contact you when I am in the town, but not in school hours of course!" answered his father. His mum smiled.

"That means I shall try to go to the town too, so that I can talk to you as well," she said. "Now let's all sit down to supper. It's your favourite meat loaf, followed by chocolate pudding!"

After supper Luke's father took the Bible down from the shelf and opened it at Psalm 121.

"I think we should read this together," he said, "I call it the Traveller's psalm."

The words seemed to come alive to Luke as his dad read the verses. He especially loved the end of the psalm where it said,

"The Lord watches over you—the Lord is your shade at your right hand; the sun will not harm you by day, nor the moon by night. The Lord will keep you from all harm—he will watch over your life; the Lord will watch over your coming and going both now and for evermore."

When Luke went to bed he found his own Bible and read the words again, then decided to underline them, so that he would always know they were special. The Bible had to go into his case, so he also wrote the words out on a bit of paper and shoved it into the pocket of his trousers which he would be wearing for the journey to school. Then, as he lay in bed, somehow the fears he had been feeling melted away and he fell fast asleep.

Chapter two

Other people were preparing for the flight to Kenya that day, too. Joel the pilot had been busy most of the day, making the necessary checks on the plane, preparing his flight schedule and loading some freight which he was taking over to Kenya along with his passengers. He always enjoyed doing the 'school run' as he called it. He loved being around children. He hoped that one day he would get married and have a family of his own.

Joel was a young New Zealander, who had always dreamt of being a pilot. After his training he had joined a missionary organisation and was posted to the centre of Congo. Sometimes, he flew supplies to other missionaries who lived in remote places, not just in the Congo, but other east and central African countries. From time to time he had to fly a doctor out to a remote place to attend to a medical emergency, or collect a patient who needed to go to a big hospital. It always felt good to help save someone's life and Joel had learnt quite a bit about first aid and medical procedures from the doctors.

"If I wasn't a pilot, maybe I would train as a doctor," he told his co-pilot George, one day. He and George took it in turns to do 'on call' shifts for such emergencies, but George had a wife and a family, so Joel would volunteer to fly the longer trips which meant a few days away from the base, such as the flights to Kenya.

The mission had two planes, Cessna Caravan 208, which could carry 8–10 passengers and also a Cessna 206 which was smaller with a piston type engine. This was the plane which Joel would fly in the morning as he only had four passengers to collect.

Just before he went to bed that night, Joel checked his passenger list. First he would fly to Central African Republic to collect two American children, Katie Ann and Paul Junior Gates, then from a Congo outpost, Luke Masters, who was British and finally, from Rwanda, a Dutch girl called Julienne Van Stamm.

"What a cosmopolitan group we will be!" Joel thought to himself. He had estimated the times to reach each place and the fuel needed, including the ongoing flight through Uganda to the Kenya Highlands, landing on an airstrip near the Hilltop International High School.

With a prayer, Joel committed the trip to God and went to sleep, ready for an early start.

In C.A.R. (as Central African Republic is known) Katie Ann and Paul Junior were also preparing for the new school term. Katie Ann was thirteen and her brother, twelve. They were used to flying off to school and both loved it at Hilltop.

Even so, it was always a bit hard to leave their parents behind, their little brother and their pets. Because they lived in such a remote place their parents had no phone or internet access and although they did write letters, sometimes they took weeks to arrive. However, their parents were hoping to visit them at half term, as they were going to attend meetings in Nairobi around that time, so the children had something exciting to look forward to. Paul had promised to try to stay out of trouble. He always seemed to get into scrapes at school and had more detentions than anyone else in his class!

Katie Ann missed her friends a lot when she was on holiday. The past couple of days she had been baking and filling her tuck box with treats which she could share with her friends. She had learnt to make some toffee, called peanut brittle and it had turned out really well.

She and her mum had also crystallised some pineapples, which should keep and be a really special treat for everyone.

In Rwanda, Julienne had also packed her bags ready for the new school term. She didn't much like school. Almost everyone spoke English at Hilltop, which she still found a bit difficult, for Dutch and French were her native languages. The school mostly had children whose parents were missionaries, but her dad was a lecturer at the university and her mum taught health education in a school. They weren't interested in God or the church or things like that, so sometimes Julienne found she didn't understand what her school friends were so excited about. She found the school chapel services and the Bible class all a bit boring. Often she wished her parents had stayed in Holland, but there were some exciting things about living in Rwanda, especially in the capital, Kigali. Julienne was looking forward to her thirteenth birthday, which was just before Christmas. She was sure that being a teenager would be great fun!

"I wonder what presents I'll get," she thought to herself, "I wonder if mum and dad will make a trip to Kenya to see me." Julienne owned all the latest gear and gadgets, far more than most of her school friends. She knew that in lots of ways she was spoilt because she was the only child of parents who had a good income.

Her mum and dad had promised that they would think about sending her back to school in Holland when she was fourteen. She wanted to live with her auntie, uncle and cousins for they were always doing exciting things and visiting exciting places. Julienne wanted to be an exciting sort of person, wanted to be beautiful, popular and have everyone look up to her and admire her. She hadn't yet decided on any particular career, but she had already decided she would be somebody important.

In her hand luggage Julienne had packed her new laptop which her parents had just bought. She could email them every day or speak on Skype, as well as on her mobile. She was grateful about that for many of her school friends couldn't contact their parents because they lived in such remote places.

"The weather forecast is quite good," her father told her that evening. "The rains are about to begin, but there aren't too many thunder storms around, so you should get a good flight. We'll leave for the airport at 7.00 am. You'd better have an early night, but first, I think we'll all go out to the Chinese Restaurant for a goodbye meal."

"Great!" Julienne exclaimed, "My favourite place to eat!"

Dressed in her new jeans and best top, she went out with her parents, had her favourite lemon chicken dish, then as soon as she was home went up to bed, falling to sleep with the sound of her favourite pop group singing on her CD player.

Chapter three

The next morning Joel was awake before it was light. He was glad that he lived in a town where there was electricity so that he could wash and shave in hot water, make coffee and be ready for his trip. He was singing to himself as he dressed. He heard his house helper Petero arrive and begin to cook breakfast.

"It is a good day for you to fly," Petero said, "I will make you a fine breakfast, so that you will not arrive hungry in Kenya and people will not say that your helper doesn't feed you well!"

Joel chuckled at Petero's speech.

"You know, Petero, that you feed me so well that I need to buy bigger trousers!" he answered. "Please look after the house for me while I'm gone and feed the chickens and the dog. I expect to be home tomorrow, but it's so good to know you are around just in case there is a delay. You truly are my 'rafiki'. (Rafiki means 'friend' in Kingwana.)

Joel glanced at his watch and decided he not only had time to read his Bible and pray but also to email his parents in New Zealand before he set off. That morning he sensed that God was very close to him as he prayed for the children who would be his passengers and also that he would pilot the plane well. As he thought about the children, he remembered he had promised Paul Junior an old book which he was given as a boy about survival in the jungle. He pushed it into his back pocket and set out with his small overnight bag to the little airport.

Everything went to schedule and soon Joel had clearance to take off from his base in Bunia. As the Cessna soared into the air, Joel thought how suitable the Congolese name, 'bird' was for a plane. Even though the plane was full of fuel, there was little cargo and no passengers so it seemed light and flew through the air like a bird. Joel had his course set for C.A.R. because his first stop was to pick up Katie Ann and Paul Junior in the capital city of Bangui. Joel took the route which followed the river Oubangui and arrived at the airport on schedule. The landing was smooth and as his flight was not a commercial one, Joel had been directed away from the main terminal to a much smaller building, where his passengers were waiting with their parents.

"Hi guys," Joel called out to the children, "All set for the trip?" Katie Ann and Paul Junior were pleased to see Joel again and while he weighed their luggage their mum poured out a welcome cup of coffee, from a thermos flask, for him to drink.

"Have you got room by any chance, for a couple of chickens?" asked Paul Senior.

"No problem," replied Joel, "Who are they for?"

"Actually, they are for the school farm," answered Paul, "They need some more stock and the hen is a very good layer, so I'm sending her along with a cock. Can you invoice the flight to me along with the children's fares?"

"Sure, I'll ask the office to see to that," replied Joel. As soon as he had finished his coffee, the parents began to help him load the baggage into a pod under the belly of the aircraft where there was extra storage room. It had to be arranged carefully, to keep the plane well balanced. Then, after hugs and kisses, the children were strapped into their seats ready for the plane to take off.

It was always a bit chaotic at Bangui, but Joel had allowed time for this; eventually the control tower told him that they could take off and he taxied down the runway and once again they soared into the air.

This time he flew east, back over the border into Congo and out to the small village of Mbethy, landing carefully on the grass landing strip. It seemed as if everyone in the area had come to see the plane! People were running from all directions and in a cloud of dust a car drove out to where the plane had landed. Inside was Luke and his parents.

"Hi, I'm Joel," the pilot introduced himself, "You must be Luke. It's your first school run, isn't it? I'm sure you'll enjoy it. Come inside and meet Katie Ann and Paul Junior. You'll sit next to Paul for the flight."

Luke was looking very nervous and gave his mum and dad one last hug before walking up the steps into the plane. His dad helped to load the luggage, this time into the plane, behind Katie Ann to keep things nicely balanced.

"I hope you have a good flight," said Luke's dad to Joel. "We've been getting a few storms this past couple of days, they can be very nasty at this time of year."

"Yes. I think it's more stormy over here in the east, but we only have one further pick up down in Kigali, then it's a straight flight over to Kenya," replied Joel, "In no time at

all I'll be bringing Luke back for the Christmas holidays—
he'll love school, I'm sure," he added, seeing how worried
they both looked. Joel realised how hard it was for parents
to send their children so far away to school.

Inside the plane, he checked Luke was settled in the
seat next to Paul.

"You have got your passport and yellow fever certificate
ready for entry into Kenya, haven't you?" he asked Luke.

"Yes Joel," Luke answered, "They are in my blazer
pocket."

"Good, then seatbelts fastened everyone, next stop
Rwanda!"

Luke's parents drove off the airstrip as Joel put the
steps away and locked the door, started the engine and
prepared to take off. There was no control tower here, so
he could immediately taxi down the air strip and back into
the skies with everyone on the ground waving them away.
Out of the little window Luke could see Manweli holding
his dog, Shenzi and he felt a huge lump in his throat.

"I mustn't cry. I'm big enough to go away to school. It's
going to be alright," he said to himself.

It seemed that Paul Junior understood, for he squeezed
Luke's hand.

"It's OK buddy. I feel the same every time I leave home,
but Hilltop High is a real cool school. We have loads of
fun. I'll look out for you. Like a bit of peanut brittle? Katie
Ann cooked it yesterday."

Luke nodded and was soon sucking the toffee which
made him feel much better. He looked out of the window
and was amazed to see the village below him getting
smaller and smaller as they climbed higher into the sky.

"Everyone alright back there?" asked Joel from the cockpit.

"Fine, thanks," the children shouted back.

"Make sure you keep the seat belts on all the time. When we get to Kigali you'll be able to have a little walk and a drink while I refuel. We're picking up Julienne, then next stop is school! Joel informed them.

"Now how about a sing song to help us along?" he suggested. Katie Ann and Paul were used to this on trips with Joel and began singing 'One man went to mow' lustily. Soon Luke was joining in and feeling much more cheerful.

Chapter four

As the plane approached Kanombe Airport in Kigali, the capital of Rwanda, once again, Joel told the children to prepare for landing and to have their passports at the ready for inspection, as they were going to be allowed into the transit lounge while the plane was prepared for the onward flight. Luke was excited. He felt very grown up entering through the arrivals door and showing his passport. Joel led the children into a lounge where Julienne and her parents were waiting for them. They had just greeted each other when Joel's mobile phone rang.

"Hi," said his colleague George. "I'm really sorry, but I need to divert your flight. I need you to fly back to Congo and collect a patient who has a medical emergency, in Beni. It's not far off your route. Please fly him to Nairobi before you go on to Hilltop, where an ambulance will get him to Hospital. Can you do that?"

"I guess so," answered Joel, "I'm refuelling here and we are well on time. Can you advise Nairobi of our time of expected arrival and the School about our delay? I can take the patient, but not much extra luggage. I have a couple of chickens extra as it is!"

"Ok. Will do," agreed George, "Have a good flight."

While Joel oversaw the refuelling and rescheduled his log book, Luke, Katie Ann and Paul Junior had drinks and snacks to keep them going. Luke was introduced to Julienne, but she wasn't very interested in a ten year old boy, but was far more interested in showing off her new laptop to Katie Ann.

It wasn't long before they were ready to take off once again. Julienne said her last goodbyes to her parents, who promised to visit her at half term and take her out to Nairobi for the long weekend then they all boarded the aircraft and settled back into their seats, the girls sitting together on one side and the boys on the other. Joel had explained that they had to fly over the Virunga volcanoes back into the Congo in order to collect the sick man from Beni, but it would only be a small delay and should be interesting for them to fly over the mountains.

Once they had clearance from the air traffic control tower, they took off, gradually rising over the city of Kigali and heading north back to Congo.

"What a lovely city Kigali looks," Katie Ann remarked to Julienne, "Look at all the tree lined highways and nice buildings!"

"Yes," answered Julienne, "I 'spose it's all right, if you have to live somewhere in the middle of Africa. At least there are a couple of good shopping malls and some decent restaurants and hotels with swimming pools. It's not much fun being a teenager here, though. I want to return to Holland and really have fun! Don't you want to be normal and live in America?" she asked.

"I've never thought about it that much," admitted Katie Ann, "I've lived most of my life in C.A.R. and although it's a poor country, I've always felt it was my home. When we go to the States for home assignment, I always feel like a stranger there and am glad to get back to Africa. Maybe I'll feel different when I have to go back for college, but that's years away!"

In the cockpit Joel was watching the weather carefully. There seemed some very dark clouds ahead and he was a bit concerned about a storm. It wasn't easy to fly through the mountains in a thunder storm.

As they flew near the town of Gisenyi, Joel pointed out Lake Kivu to the children and told them to watch out for the crater of Nyragongo volcano, which was still active and a real spectacle from the air.

The children were all amazed at the sight, even Julienne expressed wonder. Then the storm hit them. It was scary for them all. Joel was praying that he would be able to make good judgements and fly safely. He turned the plane to fly east under the shelter of the next volcano, Karisimbi and on towards the town of Muzanze where he knew there was a landing strip if the storm grew worse, but as they travelled, they flew out of the storm, so once again were able to turn north and fly over the Sabinyo volcano towards Beni.

Joel was thanking God for his help and the children were settling down again and chatting happily when disaster struck! Suddenly, the engine seized up and the propeller stopped working, so that Joel had no forward thrust. They were flying over the volcano and underneath them was dense forest. Joel struggled to see through his windscreen as oil had blown on to it and he feared the worst. The plane's engine had failed, possibly due to a broken piston rod. Joel knew his only option was to make an emergency crash landing. But, with only seconds to make any decision he cried out to the Lord for help, yelled at the children to curl up in the brace position and pray for help.

The children were already terrified, instantly obeying his command. For one second, the windscreen cleared just enough for Joel to see a plateau ahead and he made straight for it.

It was a miracle, for in the middle of what had seemed impenetrable forest, he had managed a crash landing.

"Everyone, out as quickly as possible, leave everything behind. We have leaked oil and the plane may catch fire!" he told the children, reaching for an axe by his door and breaking windows so that the children could get out and run for safety.

Julienne started to reach for her lap top.

"I said leave everything!" shouted Joel, "Your life is more important!" so reluctantly Julienne climbed out of the window and ran.

"Thank you God!" he breathed, as they all ran as far from the aircraft as they could. At least, most of them ran. Joel realised that Katie Ann was hobbling, tears running down her face. Joel ran to her and picked her up, almost slinging her over his shoulder and ran with her to the shelter of a rock.

They all crouched together, shaking with fear and shock. Looking at the wrecked plane.

"What'll happen to us?" asked Paul Junior, "Will someone come and find us?"

Although he was very shocked and frightened, Joel knew he had to take charge and be calm.

"First, we are going to pray and thank God that we are all alive and somehow landed safely. When I realised what was happening I asked the Lord to help us and save us and suddenly, the windscreen cleared just for a second or two and I saw this spot where we could make a crash landing. Let's thank God for that. Let's ask him to help us now."

The missionary children were all used to praying and happy to do that. Julienne had other ideas.

"That's stupid," she said, "You must have made a mistake and that's why we're in this mess! We're lucky to be alive. Wait until my father finds out! You wouldn't even let me collect my laptop! My father is a clever professor. He'll sue you for this! I told him I wanted to go back to Holland for school. If I had, this would never have happened to me!"

The others were shocked at Julienne's outburst.

"How can you say things like that?" said Paul Junior. "Joel is a great pilot. We should be real grateful we are alive. Joel's right, we need to pray!"

Joel led the children in a prayer, thanking God that they had survived and asking for help.

Then he looked at Katie Ann's foot. It was very swollen and definitely was an odd shape. Joel feared that it was broken. No wonder the poor girl was as white as a sheet and tears rolling down her cheeks. He knew that he had first aid equipment in the plane, but had to let the engine cool and make sure it was safe before he attempted to get things.

Joel explained this to the children and told them they would all have to help Katie. He also told them he needed to make a plan. He wanted their ideas, knowing that it would help them to be positive.

As they were thinking they heard a clucking noise and they all just had to laugh! Clucking a great deal and walking towards them were the chickens, which had somehow escaped from their cage and followed the children to safety!

Chapter five

The laughing somehow eased the terror and tension which they all were feeling. Even though Katie Ann wasn't able to get up and catch the chickens, she called softly to them, and they came clucking to her side. She often looked after the poultry at home and loved them, knowing them all as individuals.

"I'm real glad you're safe," she said to them, "I would have hated to think you might have been burnt alive in the plane."

"Now," said Joel to the children, "We need to think about what we are going to do. We have to work together as a team and make plans to help us survive until we are rescued. I will be the team leader, but you all will have to promise to do as I say and to work together."

The children all nodded in agreement.

"We need to agree on what is important," continued Joel, "Like finding food and shelter".

"Surely, a search party will be sent out quickly once we don't arrive at Nairobi airport—we won't need to sleep out here, or anything horrible like that?" exclaimed Julienne.

"I hope not," replied Joel, "But even though people will start searching as soon as they find they cannot contact us, we are in a very remote place in the middle of a forest in the mountains. It may take a while for helicopters or planes to locate us. We have to make plans in case it takes longer than we would like."

"I guess we could turn out our pockets and see what we have with us," suggested Paul Junior.

"Good idea," said Joel, "That's what we need, all of us thinking and working together."

They searched their pockets. Paul produced the rest of his bag of peanut brittle, a bit of string, a catapult, a pen and a notebook and a hanky.

"What you got buddy?" he asked Luke.

"Not much, I'm afraid," Luke answered, "My uniform is all new and apart from my passport and new phone, I just have a piece of paper that I wrote out a Psalm I wanted to remember. It seemed important to do that."

"Fat lot of good that will be!" scoffed Julienne.

"Julienne, we are working as a team and everything from everyone is important," Joel reminded her gently. "Do you want to read it to us Luke, or is it too private?"

Luke was a little embarrassed, especially being the youngest and not really knowing anyone very well.

"Last night my dad read this Psalm at supper and it seemed so special—as if God was speaking the words to me, so I copied it out. Dad calls it the 'Travellers' psalm." Luke paused for breath, then unfolded the piece of paper and read what he had written to them all.

Psalm 121
I lift up my eyes to the hills—
Where does my help come from?
My help comes from the Lord,
The Maker of heaven and earth.

He will not let your foot slip—
He who watches over you will not slumber;
Indeed, he who watches over Israel
Will neither slumber nor sleep.
The Lord watches over you—
The Lord is your shade at your right hand;
The sun will not harm you by day,
Nor the moon by night.
The Lord will keep you from all harm—
He will watch over your life;
The Lord will watch over your coming and going
Both now and forevermore.

Luke folded up the paper again and looked at everyone.

"That is the most wonderful gift you could ever have given us!" said Joel, "You have given us hope, because you have brought us God's promises. Thank you so much. Keep that piece of paper safe, we may need to read it over and over again."

Katie Ann didn't have much in her pockets either. She found some chewing gum. A pencil and a drawing book, because she loved drawing and usually kept those things with her. She also had some elastic hair bands and some tissues.

Then it was Julienne's turn. "If only you had let me bring out my handbag," she said grumpily to Joel, "I would have had lots of things! All I have is some lipstick and a nail file. They won't help much! Can you do any better?" she asked Joel.

Joel suddenly remembered that he had put a book in his back pocket to give to Paul. He pulled it out and said in a wondering voice.

"Isn't that strange? I had put this book in my back pocket to give to you, Paul. I'd been given this when I was a kid in New Zealand and thought you might enjoy it. The title is, "How to survive in the Jungle," Maybe it will help us!"

Joel also had a penknife, a pen, hanky and a packet of peppermints in his pockets.

"Well, this is quite a useful collection," he said. "A good start to our survival kit."

It's now over half an hour since we landed. Let's pray together and then I'm going down to the plane to see what we can rescue from it. I think it's safe to do that now. Once I've inspected it, then you can come and help me.

Even Julienne closed her eyes as Joel began to pray. First he thanked God so much for keeping them all alive. Then he thanked God for reminding them of his promises in the psalm and asked that they would be kept safe and Katie Ann's ankle would heal and that they soon would be rescued. Everyone said 'Amen' with feeling and really meant it from the bottom of their hearts.

Joel left the children making a list of things to do and things they would all need to survive, while he returned to the plane. He had tried to be upbeat with the kids and keep their spirits up, making out that they would have a great adventure together, but inwardly he was very worried. He knew they had crashed in a very remote place and the chances of them being found were very slim. He felt very responsible for the four children.

The main body of the aircraft was intact, but the wings had broken in the crash and there were bits of debris everywhere. A quick inspection revealed what he had feared was the most likely cause of the crash—a broken piston rod in the cylinder of the engine. He thanked God that it was a mechanical failure and not a pilot's error.

The pod under the belly of the aircraft had been damaged and that was how the chickens had escaped, but Joel was relieved to see that the spare tank of water carried there was still intact. Water was so vital for their survival! He also retrieved a box of tools which he kept in the pod and the luggage which had been stored there.

Then he made his way to the cabin and took out as much luggage and personal belongings as he could. Next he inspected the lining of the cabin. He knew that this could be ripped out to make a temporary shelter. That would be his next job.

Joel then retrieved the first aid box, which was also in good shape. He needed to strap Katie Ann's ankle. He was very glad that he had worked for his First Aid certificate before leaving New Zealand.

Oil had leaked from the turbo prop engine all over the ground, making dark streaks in the grass, and also making it slippery.

Once Joel had retrieved everything he could from the wrecked plane, he called the boys to come and help him take the things to the large rock where they were sheltering. It was a black volcanic rock with an overhanging ledge and could certainly be made into a shelter for the night.

Luke and Paul ran down to help, followed by Julienne who only seemed interested in finding her own things.

"We all need to help each other," Joel said to her, "Please take some of Katie Ann's things up to the rock." She pulled a face and picked up one extra bag and began to take it with her.

When all the bags and packages were at the rock, they decided to see how much food they had between them. By now they were all pretty hungry! They could have eaten it all at once, but Joel cautioned them that they needed to make it last as long as possible. The children were glad that they had tuck boxes in their baggage and also pleased that they could have a drink of water. They felt hot and steamy after the thunder storm.

"Don't you think that we should make a fire so that anyone looking for us might see the smoke?" suggested Paul. "It says that in the book you gave me."

"Excellent idea," answered Joel, "But we must make it well away from the plane. While I bandage Katie's ankle, will you three collect any pieces of wood that we can burn. Please stay together and within earshot because we haven't yet explored the territory around us. Just look for twigs and dry grass for they will burn easily."

They were on a plateau, which once must have been a river bed, but was really quite a small area surrounded by steep slopes which were very thickly wooded and seemed to have no tracks or paths to follow. The children scoured the area picking up anything which they thought would make a fire and began to build a bonfire as far away from the wrecked plane as possible.

Katie Ann had been very brave and tried not to complain about the pain in her ankle. It was very swollen and a funny shape. Joel felt at it carefully, a little unsure whether it was broken or just badly sprained. In the first aid box there were crepe bandages and support bandages, so Joel was able to use these to help her. He also found some pain killing tablets and gave her two. He placed the ankle on a cushion made from one of the bags, so that it was more comfortable. The chickens were clucking around her and then much to her delight, the hen produced an egg!

"I wish I could help everyone," she said tearfully, "but at least the hen has laid an egg for us!"

Chapter six

Once the fire was built, Joel soaked a piece of paper in the spilt engine oil and put it among the bits of wood and grass. Then, in the way he had learnt in the Boy Scouts years ago, he rubbed two dry sticks together until they sparked and made a flame. Somehow, the fire cheered them all. Maybe a search for them was already under way and their fire would be spotted. As they sat around the fire they felt warmer too, for it had become cold in the mountains which were damp and misty. By now it was late afternoon and Joel knew he needed to get the shelter built before darkness fell. In the tropics that happens suddenly and although they had torches in their luggage, he didn't want to waste the batteries.

Paul and Luke helped Joel to rip off some of the lining from the aircraft and drag it up to the rock. They managed to make a sort of shelter and then put on as many clothes as they could to keep warm. Amongst some of the freight, which had been in the plane, was a large African round cooking pot called a 'sufaria'. In this they were able to boil some water which they then passed around in the only two mugs they had between them, but they were able to have a hot drink. Washing was forbidden! The water was too precious. The boys thought that was great, but both girls longed to wash their faces. Finally, just before they settled, Joel asked Luke to read Psalm 121 again, to remind them that God was looking after them. They prayed together for protection through the night and finally, even though none of them thought they would, they all fell asleep.

When the plane had not arrived either at Beni or in Nairobi, the alarm had been raised.

The weather was bad all over the region with severe thunder storms that often marked the start of the rainy season. It was also getting dark, by the time the news had reached base that the plane was missing, so a search could not be mounted that day. The last direct contact had been in Kigali, when the plane had taken off, so it wasn't known exactly where the plane might have crashed, but it was most likely to have been in the Virunga mountain range. However, that was a vast area to search. Plans were made for a plane and helicopter to search the next day.

Julienne's parents were the first of the families to hear the bad news, since they could be reached by phone. They were so shocked and worried and kept wishing they had listened to their daughter's plea and sent her back to Holland instead of Kenya for her schooling.

"I'll never forgive myself," said her mother, who was sobbing her heart out, "I wish you'd never taken this job. I wish we'd never come to Rwanda!"

"Do you think I feel any different?" replied her father crossly. "You always blame me, as if everything is my fault! All I want is for our daughter to be found safe and sound."

Not knowing what to do, Julienne's father kept pestering the authorities to begin a search, even though it was now dark. Somehow, it helped to get angry and blame someone else, because he felt so helpless. The family had a few colleagues in Rwanda, but not really many friends so they didn't know where to turn. They did, however, have a Rwandan housekeeper called Ruth, who when she heard about the missing plane suggested praying about the situation. At first, Julienne's parents dismissed the idea because they didn't really believe in God, but then, in her despair, Julienne's mother agreed. She and Ruth sat together in the kitchen and Ruth prayed. Julienne's mother hadn't even been to church since she was a child and was very surprised to find, after the prayer, that she felt more peaceful, as if a big bundle had been lifted off her shoulder. Somehow, she knew at that moment that God was real and had heard their prayer.

It took much longer to get the news to both Luke's parents in Congo and Katie Ann and Paul Junior's parents in C.A.R. Both families lived in places which had no mobile phone reception or internet access. They had to rely on short wave radio to receive urgent messages and the radio didn't work so well at night or in thunder storms. It was early the next morning before these families heard the bad news. The announcement was sent all over the mission network where soon messages were coming in from friends and colleagues sending their love and promising their prayers. They were comforted to know that a search party had now been sent out.

"How glad I am that we read Psalm 121 together," commented Luke's father to his wife, "let's keep reminding ourselves that God is watching over our son."

News spreads very quickly in an African village, so before long villagers were coming to the home and sitting with Luke's parents and praying with them. Manweli came and asked if he could wait in the house until there was news of his friend and play mate. Luke's dog, Shenzi, seemed to know that something terrible had happened and wandered around with his tail between his legs, looking mournfully at everyone.

"I sure wish we could do something," Katie Ann and Paul Junior's mum said to her husband, "I'd feel a whole heap better if I could do something to help find the kids. It's awful just sitting around and waiting in case news comes on the radio network."

"Let's go and stay in town," suggested her husband, "That way we can use our mobile phones and have access to email. We can stay in the mission guest house and be on hand if we need to fly out to Kenya. You go pack some bags and I'll radio the mission office."

The couple felt better having made this decision, for they lived in a very remote place. They needed to cross a river to get to the town and in the rainy season it was very full and fast flowing so it was extremely scary crossing the plank bridge. As the rains had just started they felt it was wiser to go sooner rather than later, especially since they had their youngest little boy Sammy, with them. He was only three.

It was a very difficult time of waiting for all three families. George, the other pilot had the very difficult task of telephoning Joel's parents in New Zealand to inform them that the plane which their son was flying was reported missing in the mountains and forests somewhere between Rwanda, Congo or maybe even Uganda. Soon, people all over the world were praying about the pilot and four children who were missing.

Chapter seven

The next morning Joel and the children woke as daylight crept into their shelter. They were all stiff, cold and hungry. The sun was shining with no sign of storm clouds and they could hear birds singing in the nearby forest.

"We need to get the fire relit," Paul said, "I'm sure people will be coming to look for us this morning."

"Yes, we'll do that at once," Joel agreed, "You and Luke go searching for more fuel. Stay together and don't go far. Look in my tool bag for the panga (an African scythe) so you can cut down small branches with it, but be careful!"

"Maybe, I could cook the eggs?" suggested Julienne. She wasn't a very good cook because they had always employed a housekeeper both in Holland and Rwanda as her mother hated housework and was always busy teaching in school or at night school.

"There's another two eggs which the hen has laid," Katie Ann said. "What a blessing we have her! You could make scrambled eggs or an omelette with them. Then we can share it out. I wish I could help, but I still can't stand very well," she added.

"How's your ankle doing?" asked Joel.

"Actually, it's heaps better since you strapped it. If I try to stand, though, it still hurts a lot."

"If it's that much better then I think it may be a bad sprain, rather than a brake. That's good news." Joel replied.

He was looking at maps of the area and trying to work out where they might be. They weren't very detailed, but with his knowledge of the flight paths he could roughly work out the area in which they had crashed. He had rescued a compass from the plane, which was also a help. Joel had already decided that should they not get rescued that day, so long as Katie Ann was able to hobble on her ankle, then the next day they ought to try to find a route over the mountain and back to civilisation. It was a horrible thought, but Joel knew they could not survive long where they were once their supply of cookies, cakes and candy had been eaten.

The two boys came back with a lot of brushwood and some news.

"We saw a monkey in the trees!" said Luke, "Paul thought that if he had his catapult maybe he could try and catch it or maybe a bird. We will need meat to eat."

Julienne pulled a face. "Monkey!" she shouted at the boys, "You can't eat things like that! It's too horrible to even think about!"

Joel calmed them all down. "Just now, we'll have eggs and cookies for breakfast. We have some pineapples, too. The first animal we will kill to eat will have to be the cockerel. The hen is good at laying eggs, so we'll try not to kill her. We'll think about other meals later on."

Julienne might not have cooked an omelette before, but with Katie Ann's directions she made a very good job of it and everyone praised her. She blushed pink with happiness. She wasn't used to helping people or doing useful things and it felt so good to be thanked. It tasted the nicest food she had ever eaten. They all drank some water and carefully cleaned the cooking pan and the knife they had used in as little water as they could. It was important not to waste a drop!

After breakfast Julienne surprised them all by asking for the Psalm to be read out again. Luke took it out of his pocket. They all thought about the words. God had promised his protection by day and night. It was good to be able to talk together about how scared they really felt and frightened that they might not be rescued or ever see their families again. It was even better to pray together and ask God to look after them and help them to make wise decisions.

Joel suggested that they explore the whole of the plateau area. He could see that it was larger than he had first thought. He told the children that he was trying to work out from his maps and readings roughly where they might be, so that if need be they might be able to walk to safety.

First, he went back to the plane to see if there was something which he could make into a walking stick for Katie Ann. Not only did he find a good piece of wood which would make a really strong stick, but in the pod he also found a picnic basket which someone must have left behind, or maybe it belonged to George. It contained knives, forks, spoons, cups, plates and some water bottles. What a find! Joel knew it would make such a difference to them all at meal times. He searched around to see if there were any more useful things.

Katie Ann was very brave and tried to walk with the stick, so that she could explore the plateau, too. For a while, Joel gave her a piggy back, but she was too heavy to be carried all the time. There was no sign of any cultivation or habitation. Joel had hoped that perhaps it might have been an area which the pygmies used from time to time. At the far end the plateau shelved very deeply into a ravine. Joel shuddered to think what might have happened if he had not landed when he did. They would have had no chance of survival! However, as they peered down, they realised that there was a lake far below them.

"Well, we know there is water, even if it might prove a long, difficult trek to reach it," Joel commented.

"Maybe it's fed from a river," Paul said. "Don't most lakes have rivers flowing into them?"

"I think so," answered Katie Ann, "I seem to remember from geography lessons that there are a lot of rivers in these mountains. We must be somewhere near the Rwenzori mountain range, you know, the Mountains of the Moon, where things grow far bigger than anywhere else!"

"This is called the Great Lakes area, too," Julienne remembered. "How I would love to find a lake and have a swim and feel clean again and wash my hair!"

"Girls!" Paul said in disgust to Luke, "As if a bit of dirt mattered!"

Once they had explored all around the plateau, Joel was sure that the only way they could get out would be to trek through the forest. There was no way they could climb down the ravine. Only experienced mountaineers could do that, not four young children, with one of them injured. Had he been alone, he might have tried that idea, but there was no way he would leave the children by themselves. They would all stay together whatever happened.

The children became more and more disappointed as the day wore on and there was no sight or sound of any rescue plane or helicopter. They had managed to keep the fire alight all day and as the afternoon wore on, Joel decided they needed to start the forest trek the next day.

"We have to be brave and leave this camp tomorrow," he told them. "We need to move on before we run out of water. Water is more important than food and we now have some bottles in which to put it. I am going to kill the cockerel and then we will cook it. What we don't eat today we will carry with us for tomorrow. We'll try to take the hen with us. Maybe she'll still lay us some eggs! I want you to take only essentials with you in a back pack or bag you can sling over your shoulder. I think you all have bags like that?"

"Yes, we do," said Luke. "They are part of our school kit."

"Good. Go and think carefully. Change into sensible clothes like jeans and t shirts, but take a sweater. We need food, torches, the plates, knives and things like that. We need the tools, string and I'll try to carry the shelter and first aid box. I have a compass. We will allow just one mobile phone in case we reach somewhere with a signal. None of us must be selfish as we all need to help Katie Ann. We will put the hen in a bag and take it in turns to carry her."

"I really thought we would be found today," said Julienne. "I am scared of trekking through the forest. I want my mum and dad!" It was all she could do to stop herself from crying.

"We all feel like that," Katie Ann answered. "Even the boys, but we are all still alive and we do still have food."

"We also have the Psalm that says God will keep us from harm and watch over our lives, so however scared we are, we know we'll be alright," said Luke.

"But how do we know that the Bible is true?" asked Julienne, "It could just be a lot of myths or fairy stories. How do we know that God meant those promises for us and not for the people of long ago?"

Paul Junior stopped going through his belongings and looked at Julienne. "It's really hard to answer that question. It is all about trusting. I wish my dad was here, because he could explain better than Katie Ann or I, but often as a family we have trusted God and what he says in the Bible and he hasn't ever let us down. Maybe the four of us should make a choice that we will believe God will look after us and help us get to safety. We could hold hands and say out loud to God that we believe that what he says in this Psalm is true and we are going to trust him to get us through this adventure!"

"I think that's a good idea," answered Luke. "I can't tell you why, but when Dad read that Psalm the night before I left home, I somehow felt it was God speaking to me, that is why I wrote it out. I've never done anything like that before. I've known about God all my life, but nothing has ever been real to me before."

"I'm so glad that you did write it out, Luke," Said Katie Ann, "God knows everything, doesn't he? He knew the plane would crash and so he gave you these words to help us trust him and get through. Maybe he wants us to see it as an adventure. A sort of trusting adventure or adventure in trusting."

"OK," agreed Julienne. "I will try to believe. Let's join hands."

The four children held hands and said together, "We will trust what you say Father God, and try to believe that you will keep us from harm and watch over our lives. Amen."

Meanwhile, Joel had slaughtered the cock and was pulling out the feathers. It took him ages, even though as a child he had done things like this on his Uncle's farm. He finally had it cut into pieces and decided to cook them all, so that they could take the left over's with them for the next day's meal. He was very happy that they had some protein to eat. Afterwards, they ate the pineapples from the cargo they were taking to Kenya.

"That was the best food I have ever tasted!" said Luke, when they had finished. Everyone laughed.

"It's not really," said Paul, "It just seems like it because you're so hungry!

They all helped clear up the mess after the meal.

"Even though we seem to be in an uninhabited place, we'll leave it tidy," said Joel. They dug a small pit and buried the bones, feathers and skin of the cock. That evening they all had a small amount of water in which to wash then once again as the light faded, they all settled down to sleep."

"When I was very small I had a nanny who looked after me," said Julienne. "She used to sing me to sleep with a song that said the angels watched over me. I think the angels really may be watching over us."

"Won't you sing it to us?" asked Katie Ann, then they all drifted off to sleep as she sang a lullaby in Dutch.

"Lord, you don't sleep, but you watch over us. Thank you so much, Joel prayed as he fell asleep.

Chapter eight

The next morning everyone woke at dawn. They were stiff and cold. Joel had figured out that they were pretty high in the mountains because it was so cold. They were glad that they had some warm clothes and anoraks. The little hen had once more supplied them with enough eggs for breakfast.

"I think God is making our hen work twice or three times as hard as usual, to give us these eggs!" said Katie Ann. "It's like the story where the prophet Elijah was fed by the ravens."

"What story is that?" asked Julienne. Katie Ann told her about the prophet Elijah who lived through a time of drought and famine. She explained that every morning and evening God sent him bread and meat carried by ravens and he had water from a brook to drink. "It was a miracle that kept him alive. When the brook dried up then God sent him to a widow and did another miracle to feed them both until the drought ended." (You can read the story in 1 Kings Chapter 17.)

"That's a great story to remember," said Joel. "The Lord is looking after us. Before we start off on our trek it's good to remind ourselves again of Psalm 121. It won't be easy and at times we might be discouraged, but we are not on our own, God is with us and will look after us."

Joel and the children put the fire out and then packed all the belongings, they were not taking with them, in a neat pile under the rock. Luke had a good idea.

"Why don't we write a note and leave it with our bags, then if someone finds the wreck they will know what we are doing." He suggested.

"Everyone agreed this was a really cool idea so they added messages for their parents, sending their love.

They then set out. Joel had the biggest load to carry, as he was taking the shelter structure which he had torn from the wrecked plane, also as many tools as he could as well as a few personal belongings.

The hen was in a bag and Julienne offered to carry her as it was all Katie Ann could do to walk, using her stick.

Once they had entered the forest, it felt completely different. It was cold and misty. The sun couldn't shine through the large trees very well, so the ground was very muddy and slippery. Many of the trees had very large broad leaves and some of them had puddles of water on them.

"We might be able to pour water from those leaves into our bottles if we run out of the other water," suggested Paul. It was a possibility and cheered them all up as they knew they needed water, above all else, to survive.

Joel had to use the panga, to cut a way through the lower undergrowth. He went first and then the children followed. There were noises in the trees above them. They heard birds singing, but also rustling in the branches, which was eerie and made them feel as if they were being watched.

Joel was glad he had a compass which he had set, so he decided they would try to walk south. That way, he hoped they might get down the mountain and into Rwanda. He felt that would be the best way back to civilisation. The going was slow and very tiring.

"I keep getting stung by these huge stinging nettles!" complained Luke, "They are stinging me through my jeans!"

"Me, too, buddy," replied Paul Junior, "I've never seen so many!"

"It tells me that we are really high up," answered Joel, "But there is one thing about them. We can use them as a vegetable. They make good soup and taste like spinach."

"Ugh!" remarked Julienne, "It sounds just horrible!"

"We may have to eat things we don't like in order to keep alive," Joel told her.

Katie Ann was very quiet. It took all her energy to try and keep up with the others and she was quite short of breath. The cold, damp air seemed to hurt her lungs every time she took a breath. She wasn't sure which was worse, the pain in her chest or the pain in her ankle. She didn't want to make a fuss or worry the others, but was really glad when Joel called out to them that they could rest for a bit.

Not that it was easy to find anywhere suitable but they had reached a place where a couple of branches had fallen down so at least it was somewhere where they could sit.

They were all so glad of a drink, but dared not drink too much water. They also snacked on Katie Ann's peanut brittle.

"This is the best thing I have ever tasted, Katie Ann," said Luke, "You must be the best cook in C.A.R.!"

Katie Ann tried to laugh and say she wasn't that good, but the words just wouldn't come out of her mouth properly. Joel looked at her with alarm. He noticed that her lips were rather a bluish colour and her cheeks were bright red. Her breathing was very rapid. He realised she was ill, but didn't know enough about medicine to know quite what was wrong or what he might do. He put his hand on her forehead and found it was hot.

"Maybe she has pneumonia," he thought to himself, "Sometimes people get it after a shock."

"Guys", he said to the others, "I think Katie Ann is sick. We need to find a place where we can make a shelter for her to rest for a little while. I'm not quite sure what to do for the best. First, we should pray and ask Jesus to heal her. He knows we are a long way from medical help.

Then, I'll search through the first aid kit and see what there is in there that might help."

The children gathered round and prayed. Paul was especially worried about his sister. He had never seen her look so ill.

"Have you taken your malaria tablets?" he asked. She nodded. "It hurts here," she tried to say, pointing to her chest."

"My Oma would make herb tea, if I had a fever," said Julienne. "Can we make a fire, boil some nettles in the water and make herb tea?" (Oma is Dutch for Grandmother.)

Glad to have a suggestion, Joel said he would take the boys and look for twigs. He knew it would be hard to get a fire lit, but he had soaked some rags in the aircraft fuel before they left the plateau for this very purpose.

Julienne stayed with Katie Ann while the others went on to see what they could find.

It was horrible to see her friend looking so ill and barely able to talk. Julienne had long forgotten to be cross about leaving all her nice things behind, but she had put a very warm sweater inside her backpack. She pulled it out and wrapped it around Katie Ann's shoulders to give her a little more warmth. She knew that even when she had been burning up with a fever, her Oma had put extra blankets around her.

'I'm frightened', Julienne thought to herself. 'Katie Ann is so ill she could die! What happens if she dies while we are in the forest?' As she sat next to the sick girl, she thought about the prayer they had just said.

'Can Jesus really be alive and make people well? Are the words in that Psalm 121 true? Will God watch over our lives?' All these questions were running through her mind. She thought about how they had held hands only yesterday and promised to trust God's Word. It had seemed more like an adventure then. She had expected they would soon walk down the mountain and through the forest to safety. This wasn't the sort of adventure she had wanted to happen!

Katie Ann was making strange noises and mumbling weird things. Julienne held her hand and decided that she really would believe and trust in Jesus.

"I don't understand much," she told Jesus, "But please, please, don't let Katie Ann die out here in the forest.

Please send some help. Please take us all safely home. I promise I will always believe in you."

Julienne thought she heard Katie mumble, "Water", so she found her water bottle and put it to her friend's lips so that she could swallow a few drops. Then Katie went quiet and it seemed she had fallen asleep.

Meanwhile, the two boys and Joel cut a trail continuing in a southerly direction, all the time looking for twigs and also a better place to make a shelter. Joel was beginning to despair when suddenly they reached a clearing in the trees. There they saw the remains of a Batwa hut. (Batwa are the pygmy people who used to live in the forest years ago.)

It was old, just a structure of woven twigs covered with leaves and grasses over a hollowed out sort of cave.

"Amazing!" said Joel, "This is just the place! Thank you Lord."

They crawled inside and found it wasn't too damp or wet. Some of the grass floor was dry and easily pulled up. It would make the basis of a fire. Joel then cut down a few branches from a tree and took the leaves off them.

"Put the leaves over the roof," he told the boys, "and build the fire with the twigs, but as far from the hut as possible. We don't want it to catch fire! Now we must go and fetch the girls." He added.

"Joel," said Paul Junior, "Luke and I will be ok here. We'll stay and build the fire ready for lighting and forage around for food."

"Are you sure?" questioned Joel. "Promise you won't leave this little area."

"Yeah, sure thing, I promise," replied Paul, looking at Luke, who nodded his head. So Joel headed back to the girls as quickly as he could.

The boys began to gather as much dry material as they could find to build a fire. They did only explore the area around the hut, always keeping it in their sight. Both of them were too scared to venture any further into the forest. They were getting a bit more used to the noises but were not sure what wildlife might be around. Luke was especially afraid of meeting a snake. His friend Manweli had told him stories of people in the village where they lived who had been bitten by poisonous snakes and had died.

The stinging nettles were still a problem, but Joel had hacked lots of them down. As they were hunting around, Luke suddenly stumbled and got entangled in something. He felt his feet get trapped and screamed out in alarm to Paul.

"My feet have got all caught up in something, can you help me?"

Paul came running over and saw that Luke had got tangled up in some sort of old net made of vines. The net was mostly covered with vegetation, but it was still quite strong. Paul helped Luke get his feet clear. He wished he had a good knife; it would have been so much easier!

"I wonder why this is here?" asked Luke, once he had recovered from his shock. "I guess it must be something to do with the hut."

"Maybe it was used to spread washing on, a sort of washing line. The women in our village spread their clothes over bushes to dry," commented Paul. "Anyway, it's very strong and when Joel gets back he could cut it down for fuel."

As they were looking closely at the net, Luke noticed there were some mushrooms growing at the base of it.

"Look Paul!" he said with excitement, "Do you think these are edible?"

Now Paul Junior still had the book which Joel had given him about survival in jungles and forests. He pulled it out of his anorak pocket.

"Let's see what his book says," he said. "They do look like mushrooms to me."

He picked one and began to peel off the skin as he had seen his mother do and smelt it too.

"We'll ask Joel, but I'm pretty sure it's ok," he said. Paul started to look further into the book.

"It tells you lots about insects and bugs you can eat. The girls won't like that!" he giggled.

"Let's go back to the hut and read more," suggested Luke, "We can take that mushroom and see what Joel thinks."

Back in the hut they were glad to sit down for a bit. It was warmer inside. They pored over the book trying to find out what food they might be able to eat.

"It says that there are many edible plants, insects, fruit and fish, but not to eat plants with white or yellow berries, plants with thorns, plants with shiny leaves or leaves in groups of three, umbrella shaped flowers, beans or plants with seeds inside a pod, have a milky or discoloured sap or anything with an almond smell."

"How can we remember all that?" asked Luke.

"I reckon we'll just have to carry the book with us and check all the time," answered Paul.

"Now here's a section on insects. Don't eat brightly coloured ones. That's easy enough to remember. Don't eat hairy insects or ones which have a pungent smell."

"What's a pungent smell?" asked Luke.

"I think it means a strong smell that tickles your nostrils or something like that," replied Paul.

"I guess we'd notice that then," Luke said adding, "Once I saw a bright red caterpillar. It looked beautiful, but the red must have been a warning sign not to eat it!"

"It says you can boil or slowly roast worms, grubs and ants!" Paul read out. "It doesn't sound very appetising, does it?"

"No, but I'm so hungry now I could eat a horse!" Luke commented.

"What a funny thing to say!" Paul Junior had never heard that expression before.

"It's what people say in England when they are really, really hungry." he answered. "Mum said they eat horses in other European countries, but the British people don't like that idea. I guess when you are starving you don't mind what you eat."

"We've been served flying ants and locusts when we've been out in the villages visiting people. Actually, they were fried in oil and tasted good—a bit like bacon."

Just then they heard voices and were very glad to know that Joel and the girls had arrived at the new camp.

Chapter nine

Joel was carrying Katie Ann, plus he had a lot of things fixed to his back pack. If the boys hadn't been so worried about Katie Ann's condition, they would have laughed because Joel looked like a funny sort of turtle!

Behind him came Julienne, also very well laden. Fortunately, the chicken seemed to have got used to her and was very quiet in her bag.

Joel carefully laid Katie Ann down in the shelter. She wasn't asleep, but was very quiet. Joel had told her to try not to talk as it hurt her chest so much. Everyone made her as comfortable as possible and Joel began to look through the first aid box to see if there was anything to help.

When he found a box labelled 'antibiotics' he was so relieved. Inside were a few packets and these had directions written on them saying, how they might best be used. One packet was for chest infections so he decided that was the best for Katie. He read the dosage carefully and gave her the first pill. It was hard for her to swallow, but she managed to get it down.

"We are going to light a fire and get some herb tea made for you," Julienne told her, "You will soon be well again." Katie Ann nodded and tried to whisper "thanks".

Joel was very interested to see the net which the boys had found and quickly cut it away, agreeing it would be very good kindling material.

"I think I know what it is," he told the children. "The Batwa people who used to live in these forests had a method of catching animals for food. They made nets and strung them up, just like this one and then some of the hunters went into the trees and made such a noise that the animals got scared and started to run. The men chased them into the net, where they were shot with bows and arrows. The fact that this net is still here would suggest that in the not too distant past there was game around here. That should encourage us. We are probably not too far from habitation and this warns us we might hear noises in the night made by animals in the area."

The fire was alight and the nettle tea brewing. Once again they looked at their rations and decided to eat Luke's cookies which his mum had made. What a blessing they had their full tuck boxes with them! If they had crashed at the end of term, they would be empty!

They had travelled only a short distance that day, but since it was already in the afternoon and they had a good place to shelter for the night, as well as Katie Ann's illness, Joel decided not to try to go on any further.

He still had the rest of the cockerel and because it was so cold in the mountains and had been well cooked the night before, Joel was sure it was still good to eat. The boys had shown him the mushroom which he tasted a little and was sure it was a field mushroom such as grew in New Zealand. He sent the children to gather some more and also look for wild celery, which grew in the mountains, that he knew the Batwa people ate. How glad he was that out of interest he had researched a little about these pygmy people and their former lifestyle. These days they mostly lived among other Rwandans and were renowned as skilled potters, but they used to live in the mountains and lived as 'hunters and gatherers' of wild game, fish, insects and berries.

The hen, who Julienne had nicknamed 'Mrs Egg' was living up to her name and producing far more eggs than any hen would normally lay. Joel told them it was a miracle because a hen would normally only lay one egg a day and it was a sign that the Lord was looking after them.

Julienne was in charge of the cooking, with Joel's supervision. She was so happy to do something useful. No one had ever trusted her to do things like cooking before. In her home there had always been housekeepers and nannies and they had treated her like a duchess. She had never been allowed to help and now she felt important because she was needed. She so wanted to help! It felt so good to be part of a team. She loved nicknaming things and so she called everyone the 'ACE SURVIVAL TEAM'.

When they tasted their stew of chicken, mushrooms, nettles and wild celery the team praised her cooking skills which made her feel so happy, even though they were lost in a thick tropical forest at the top of a mountain and nobody knew where they were!

Joel was pleased to see Katie Ann had fallen asleep. Her breathing was definitely easier. Her forehead was not so hot and he thanked God for his healing. He was concerned that it might take them several days to reach safety and they had little food and water left. At the moment the children were still cheerful, but he knew they could quickly become very worried and even give up hope of being found alive. He tried to invent games to keep their spirits up. It also helped him to keep his spirits up, too.

That evening, before they went to bed, he played a game of 'legs' with them. They went through the alphabet, naming something with legs. The person who had the most things which no one else had thought of was the winner. It kept them busy for ages. They had been really stuck on 'X' when Luke shouted out "X factor winner!" remembering a TV show in England. Everyone cheered and he was declared the winner. There was no prize, but that didn't matter.

Before they went to bed they did two things, well three really. Together they wrote a diary of all the events of the day, to have a good record to tell their parents when they saw them again. Then they read Psalm 121 to remind themselves that they were not alone, the Lord was with them and he didn't go to sleep by day or night and was watching over them. Then they talked to God, giving all their fears and worries to him, praying for their parents, thanking him for all the good things of the day like finding the hut and the mushrooms and that Katie Ann was a bit better.

The children fell asleep quickly, but Joel only dozed. He felt so responsible. He needed to wake Katie Ann every four hours and give her doses of antibiotic and drinks. She did seem to be improving, but he was still concerned. He was aware, too, that although they had buried the chicken bones from their evening meal, if there were wild animals around then these might sniff them out. At one point in the night Joel was sure he heard a hyena. Even he felt a bit scared by that. It was surprising how many noises there were in the forest through the night. It was cold, too and he had put his warm anorak over Katie Ann for the night.

He kept wondering if they would make it through the forest to safety. He only had a vague idea of their location. He had always wanted to have an adventurous life, that was why he had become a pilot, but this was just a bit too scary even for him and he had four young people to look after as well.

As he lay, tossing and turning, Joel heard a voice speaking to him. He knew it was 'in his head' but it was so very clear just as if a person was in the hut with him. He sat bolt upright. Twice the voice repeated a verse which he had often read in the Bible.

"Never will I leave you, never will I forsake you." (Hebrews chapter 13 verse 6.)

"Indeed I will never, no never leave you or forsake you!" the voice explained again.

Thoroughly awake by now, Joel searched for his torch and his Bible to look up the verse again. He noticed the next part of the verse which said,

"The Lord is my helper; I will not be afraid."

He knew that the Lord Jesus had spoken into his mind and he felt so grateful. He put out his torch to save the battery and lay down again, full of thanks to the Lord. As he lay the verse of an old hymn he had learnt back in New Zealand came back to him,

"Through the love of God our Saviour, all will be well." Singing it to himself he drifted off to sleep, knowing that God had given him the peace he needed and the courage to go on.

Chapter ten

As the hours passed, so the terrible anxiety the children's parents felt, increased. At first they were very hopeful that the search parties would soon find the missing aircraft and at least they would know what had happened to their children. It was a huge disappointment when George returned having searched the area very thoroughly with Katie Ann and Paul Junior's dad. Paul Senior was using very powerful binoculars and George flew as low as he dared over the route which he had expected Joel to take. Julienne's parents had also paid for an army helicopter to search the area, but this was unsuccessful as well.

The terrible situation brought the families together and they all decided to stay at Bunia in Congo, where George and Joel had their base. Bunia was a good sized town and had some internet and telephone access, as well as having the small airport. Katie Ann and Paul Junior's parents already knew Luke's mum and dad, but Julienne's parents didn't know anyone. Julienne's dad was angry with everyone around him for his worry was driving him crazy. When his wife joined the other parents in praying for God to help them in their search he became even angrier. He just didn't understand. He had always managed his life very well without bothering about God and had brought up Julienne in the same way. He had always thought his wife was on his side, but now she wanted to join these Christian parents in their prayers.

Julienne's mum tried to explain to him that of course she was on his side, but when the news of the loss of the aircraft first reached them, their housekeeper had prayed with her and since then even with all the worry, she felt a peace and stillness inside. It had made her realise that God was real and had listened to their cries for help. Her husband was so angry he felt like hitting his wife, but turned away muttering about her needing something like religion to prop her up, but he was strong enough on his own!

George spent as much time as he could with the parents at the hotel where they were staying. He still had to go out on flying missions when emergencies occurred but had cancelled all the routine operations. Instead of the two aircraft there was now only the Cessna Caravan. Fortunately, it was the larger of the two planes in the fleet and could carry up to ten passengers.

George managed to get hold of some very detailed maps of the Virunga mountain range and kept poring over them looking for places where the plane might have tried to land if it was in difficulties.

"My gut feeling is that they must have crashed somewhere on Mount Sabinyo," George told the parents. "I think that it might help everyone if I took you all up there tomorrow. Seeing the mountain and forest for yourselves might help you to understand what a difficult job this search and rescue mission is. Seven pairs of eyes will be better than two.

We will leave at dawn, so long as I get clearance to do a flight. Maybe you would like to get some food together and we will take a good supply of drinking water with us too, because if we find Joel and the kids, they will be short of both by now."

"Thank you George," the parents said. It was such a relief to actually be able to do something. The waiting was terrible because all of them kept thinking of what might have happened to their children.

The three mums at once decided to go to the local shops and find some suitable food.

Meanwhile the three fathers also had an idea. They decided to contact the game park rangers who worked in the area. It meant calls to Uganda, Rwanda as well as the Congo authorities. These rangers trekked through the mountains, tracking where the mountain Gorillas lived and monitoring any poaching that might be happening, as well as taking visitors on safari to see them.

When the families prepared for the next day, even Julienne's dad seemed more cheerful. Perhaps they would find the plane and perhaps their children were safe!

That evening all the parents except for Julienne's dad, spent a while praying together and once again Luke's father read Psalm 121, as he had done the night before Luke left home.

The words were so meaningful and comforting. God didn't go to sleep! He was in control and knew exactly what had happened and where the children were.

Another group of people were praying, too. In Kenya, there had been great concern when the plane bringing the children to Hilltop International High School had not arrived. Then they heard that it had disappeared and was thought to have crashed in the Virunga or the Rwenzori mountains. The school was a Christian school which had been founded originally to look after the educational needs of missionary's children so that they wouldn't have to leave Africa when they reached high school age. Years ago many children had to attend boarding schools in Europe or America and rarely saw their parents. Many families were not able to afford both school fees and then flights out for the school holidays. Hilltop High had been a wonderful solution for them. As many of the students lived in remote places and had few friends from their own cultures, the young people became very close friends at school. Prayer times in the classrooms, chapel and dormitories became focussed on asking God to help the search and rescue teams to find the four missing children and their pilot. Not all the children at the school were from mission families. There were also students from families like Julienne's who were working abroad and wanted their children to get a good education not too far away from them. Then there were some African children whose parents wanted their children to do very well in school, so that they would eventually be able to go to college in America or Europe but of course, could also afford the fees at Hilltop.

The Christian teaching at the school had helped many of the students to make a decision to love and serve the Lord Jesus and quite a few of them had already decided they would come back to Africa and be missionaries themselves.

They prayed and prayed for Katie Ann, Paul Junior, Luke and Julienne and were longing to hear some good news.

Up in the mountains their prayers were being answered. The next morning when Joel and the children woke up Katie Ann was so much better! Not only was she able to breathe without pain and her fever had disappeared but also her ankle was almost the right shape and size again! It was a miracle!

"You must keep on taking the antibiotics," Joel told her, "Just in case the infection isn't completely dealt with."

Katie Ann agreed. She didn't mind at all. It was just so good to feel better!

Once again their miracle hen was clucking away and producing eggs for them all. They all knew it had to be a miracle, because there was little for her to scratch around and eat, but she kept on laying!

Julienne took charge of the cooking once again. She now called herself the 'Ace Survival Team Cook' and boiled everyone eggs and made some more nettle tea, not even minding when her hands were stung. She was singing as she worked, sometimes in Dutch and sometimes in English. She had never felt so accepted before or had such good friends. She knew that when they got out of this forest these friends would still be her friends. Sharing this adventure had really changed her life. Why, she had almost forgotten to complain about not being able to wash and change her clothes! Somehow, that didn't seem very important any more, but learning more about God as a father who loved and cared for her, did now seem the most important thing to do!

Once breakfast was finished, they tidied up the hut fire and surrounding area, wanting to leave it just as they had found it. As they were doing this Paul Junior suddenly called out,

"Over here everyone, look at this!"

They all rushed over to him, wondering what he had seen. They stared at the mud and saw quite large paw marks.

"What made these?" Luke asked.

"I think they are from a hyena," Joel told them, "I thought I heard the cry of one in the night. I prayed we would all be kept safe. God has looked after us!"

"Wow!" said Luke, "We must put that in our safari diaries!"

Soon they were ready to start on their trek. Joel went first, slashing through the undergrowth and making a path for them all. The two girls followed next, Julienne carrying Mrs Egg in the bag and Katie Ann hobbling as best she could using the stick which Joel had made for her. She was very brave and hardly ever complained about her ankle. The two boys brought up the rear. Everyone was pretty cheerful and from time to time they sang songs to help them along the way.

Joel was just following the compass readings as much as he could, making sure they were trekking in a southerly direction. They had become used to the early mornings being cold and misty and they wore their anoraks. By the middle of the morning they had made good progress and it was getting warmer. The vegetation was changing and they saw that instead of just huge trees, they were now walking through a mixture of broad leaved trees and bamboo. The bamboo was very tall, but more sunlight was able to filter through the branches. From time to time they heard rustling and the boys were pretty sure that there were monkeys jumping from branch to branch, but they were so quick it was hard to see.

After a couple of hours of walking everyone was tired and ready for a rest. Joel thought he could hear water and decided to change direction and follow the sound. He was right. There was water! Suddenly, they came through the bamboo and saw something wonderful!

Chapter eleven

In a valley not far below them Joel and the children saw a waterfall! It wasn't huge or even very high, but just to see the water was amazing! There was a river about ten metres wide falling over a cliff which was maybe twelve or so metres high. The water looked clear and sparkling and Joel thought that it could be pure enough to boil and drink.

"Don't rush!" He warned the children. "Especially you, Katie Ann, take care going down this little gorge. It may well be slippery and we don't want any more injuries!"

They carefully made their way down to the waterfall. The vegetation had thinned out and there was more grass and bushes than dense forest. The sun was shining and for the first time they felt really warm.

"Be careful," continued Joel, "There may be more wildlife around as animals will come to drink water. Of course, this is flowing very freely, but there could be insects or snakes. Look where you are walking!"

Down by the edge of the river, underneath the waterfall there were several large boulders.

"Hurray!" said Luke, "We can sit on these. They feel really warm! Can we paddle or swim?"

"Take off your back packs and anoraks and rest a bit while I investigate. Let me see how strong the current of the river is first."

The children were only too glad to do this. Julienne had made a kind of collar and lead from string for Mrs Egg because she was afraid to let her run loose. If there were snakes they might find her a tasty snack and she was determined that that would not happen! The little hen seemed happy to stay near the children and clucked away as she pecked at the ground. There was nice fresh grass for her to eat.

Meanwhile, Joel had walked to the river bank and found a place where it was shallow enough to step down into the water. It was icy cold, but so refreshing to his feet! The water seemed to be clear and although it was flowing well, it wasn't deep. He decided it would be safe for paddling and swimming. He took a sample of the water and had a tiny sip. It tasted sweet. Joel had been a bit afraid that if it had flowed from a crater lake near the top of the volcano, then it might contain minerals which would make it unfit for drinking. This, he was sure, would be fine. It probably would be ok straight from the river, but he wasn't taking any risks. He felt sure they could find enough kindling material to light a fire, boil a whole pan full of water and allow it to cool while the children played.

Soon he was back with the children.

"This is such a good place!" he said, "The water is cold, but it's shallow and you can paddle and swim and even wash! First, can we all fill the cooking pan with water before we splash about and muddy it. Next we'll collect stuff for a fire to boil the water and then you can all have some fun."

The children were really excited at the thought of washing! Julienne had a small bar of soap in her backpack so once the fire was going and the water on to boil, they stripped to their underwear and had great fun in the water. Everyone used the piece of soap and even washed their hair. It felt so good to be clean again. Then they lay on the warm rocks and were surprised at how quickly they dried off. It was like being at the beach!

Of course, by this time, everyone was hungry again but now their supply of tuck box treats was almost finished.

"I think we should look around for food," Paul Junior suggested, pulling out his survival manual and consulting it. He read out loud to the others all about red insects and white and yellow berries.

"What about cutting some young bamboo shoots?" said Katie Ann, "After all, the Chinese eat them a lot, don't they?"

"Brilliant idea!" was Joel's comment. He had been getting worried about their food supply. "I'll go and collect some now."

"I've got an idea, too," added Julienne. "Look, there's a big snail crawling up this rock! We eat snails sometimes in Holland. They are lovely with butter and garlic!"

"I don't know about eating them," said Luke, pulling a face, "But if you say they are good to eat, I guess I'll try!"

They each took a cup and went hunting for snails. They were easy to find near the boulders and the river's edge. The problem was trying to stop them from crawling out of the cups! They realised that first they should have put a pan of water on to boil and then collected the snails!

It actually took a long time to refill the cooking pan with water from the river and find more fuel for the fire. When at last it was boiling, Julienne had taken over the task of boiling the snails and also the bamboo shoots. She had also found some more wild celery and some wild garlic. There was no butter, but you couldn't have everything! She began to think how amazing God was in the way he provided food for them!

In spite of their doubts, they all ate the snails and bamboo shoots and found them very tasty. They ate until they were absolutely full to bursting! They also drank quite a lot of their water, so Joel said they should fill the pan and boil another lot, ready to refill their water bottles before they continued their trek.

Once the water was on to boil, they felt sleepy and dozed on the warm boulders in the sun.

Luke was half asleep when he heard a noise. He wasn't sure if he was dreaming. It sounded like a plane's engine. Surely not!

He sat up and shook Paul Junior who was beside him.

"Can you hear what I can hear?" he asked in excitement. "It's a plane!" Joel had been fast asleep, he was so tired having been awake so much of the previous night. Once the children had woken him, he leapt up in excitement.

"It's a Cessna Caravan. I recognise the engine tone. I can't see it, but anyway, let's wave and yell! Someone is looking for us!"

The children didn't need to be told twice! They screamed and shouted and waved their clothes! Joel ran and stoked up the fire so that the smoke and flames would rise. They could hear the engine, but the plane didn't come near enough for them to see or be seen.

They were so disappointed! Tears trickled down the girl's faces and the boys were struggling not to cry, too. The plane had been so close! How could it have missed them!

Joel tried to comfort them. "They are still out there looking for us. Don't forget God's promise that he will watch over our lives. Let's ask him again to rescue us and bring us to safety."

Together they prayed and they all told the Lord once again that they would trust him to look after them, whatever happened.

Joel decided that to cheer them up he would give them each a piece of the peanut brittle. As they were sucking it, enjoying the sweetness, they heard another noise!

It was Mrs Egg clucking in great agitation. The children ran to where she was tethered and they were horrified to find a big snake with its head reared up ready to strike.

Joel ran to get the big stick he had cut to defend them against snakes, but meanwhile, Julienne took them all by surprise.

"How dare you!" she screamed at the snake! Then in her anger at the snake threatening their hen, she grabbed a cloth, took the pan from the fire and poured boiling water over it. It was done almost without thinking and surprised herself as well as everyone else and especially the snake! The snake looked as if it was dead, but Joel cut the head off, just to be sure.

Afterwards, Julienne was shaking with fear and shock. She had always been terrified of snakes and her biggest fear after they crashed had been that one might attack her!

"Well done Julienne," Joel praised her, "You are very brave and thought so quickly! You have not only saved the hen, but maybe us as well! What is more, you have also found our evening meal! It may not sound very nice, but we can have snake steaks this evening!"

Joel had planned that they trek further that day, but he soon realised that it might be best to camp by the river that night and continue south in the morning.

Chapter twelve

The day when the parents all went up in the Cessna Caravan they had high hopes that they might find their children and Joel. It was a bright morning, no signs of thunder storms, so visibility was good. All three of the fathers had binoculars to help them search.

They flew From Bunia down to Goma, then followed the Virunga mountain range. It was a spectacular flight, but none of the parents could really appreciate how beautiful they were. They were so intent on looking for a crashed aeroplane.

George flew as low as he could and the parents could see how dense the forests were and what a vast area they had to cover. He turned the plane from flying east to north guessing that Joel would have done that to make his diversion to collect the sick person at Beni. Whenever he saw a little river he tried to zoom in but he dared not get too low in case he became entangled with the trees. There was no sign of the missing plane.

Everyone was very disappointed, as disappointed as the Ace Survival Team were when they heard the Cessna but were not spotted by the pilot and could not make contact. George flew once more in a circle over the top of the volcano, then turned to head south towards Muzanze for one last search before returning to Bunia airport. He was crying out to the Lord in his head when he saw the small plateau between two ridges and although it was a bit risky he flew in as low as he could.

It was Luke's father who first spotted the crashed plane. He shouted to the others in his excitement.

"Look, that must be it!" he called out. George zoomed in as low as he dared, not wanting to cause another crash. There was no room for his bigger aircraft to land and he marvelled that Joel had been able to land on the small strip of level ground.

"I'll have to do another circle, then come in low again," he told the parents. "Try to see if there are any signs of life."

He slowly circled around and brought the plane as low as he could one more time. The men searched with their binoculars and Julienne's father saw the baggage stowed underneath the overhanging rock where Joel and the children had left it.

"They must have survived!" he exclaimed, "Look, their bags are neatly under that rock!"

"No one is around," answered Paul and Katie Ann's dad, "I think they must be trekking through the forest."

"Look how dense the forest is!" remarked his wife, "However will they get through it and what will they eat and drink!"

"They have their tuck boxes," answered Luke's mum, thinking how glad she was that she had made so many cookies.

"The Cessna carries water in the pod underneath it," remarked George "and I left my picnic basket there last time I flew in it, so they will have cups and water bottles.

I was so cross with myself for forgetting to take it out, but the Lord had his purpose in me leaving it behind!"

"What happens now?" asked Julienne's mother.

"We head back to base and inform the Rwandan authorities. I have the exact location from my instruments. I hope we can persuade the army to fly in a helicopter to look at the wreckage and send out rangers to that area. Thank God we have located the plane!" said George with great feeling.

"We all say 'amen' to that!" answered Luke's father and even Julienne's father agreed to that.

Although they had not found Joel and the children, everyone felt happier. Now they had hope! They hated to think of the children out in that dense forest, but they probably were still alive!

A much relieved group of passengers left the Cessna Caravan and headed towards the hotel in Bunia. They needed to do some telephoning and emailing to spread the good news and ask for help from the Rwandan government. There were no commercial helicopters to send out, so they needed the army to help.

Maybe, it was because they had been swimming or maybe, because they all felt clean again, but that night everyone in the Ace Survival Team slept soundly. They woke at dawn and Luke was the first to crawl out of the shelter they had made. The sun had just risen and the sky was an amazing pink. Luke looked down to the river and saw a wonderful sight. Playing in the waterfall and by the side of the river was a whole troupe of monkeys. They looked a golden yellow colour and there were adults and babies. He quickly and quietly woke the others.

"Shhhh!" he said, his finger over his lips, "Look over to the waterfall!"

"Wow!" whispered Joel, "They must be the golden monkeys. I have heard about them. They are a rare species which live up in these volcanoes. They are very shy creatures, so we are really fortunate to see them!"

Everybody watched as the monkeys played. Then one of them must have either seen the children or caught their scent because they suddenly all raced away and were hidden in the forest in a few seconds.

"I guess we must get breakfast and be ready to go on our way," Joel told them.

"How much boiled water have we got? We need to make sure all the water bottles are filled before we leave here."

Julienne decided to hard boil all the eggs. Mrs Egg had obliged yet again. She was a miracle hen without any doubt!

"I didn't believe in miracles or prayers being answered last week but after all that has happened to us, I know for sure that God is real and what is written in the Bible is true." She told the others as they munched on their eggs and the last few of Luke's cookies.

"Somehow, it makes all that has happened more than an adventure, for it has changed my life. I have promised to follow Jesus and live my life for him. I am sorry that I was so selfish about everything and I know now that laptops and things like that are nice, but not the really important things, are they?"

Joel looked at Julienne.

"We have all been on a steep learning curve, as the saying goes," he agreed, "We have all learnt to really trust the Lord to keep us safe and look after us. The journey isn't finished yet. It might just get harder before we reach safety, but I am sure that God will not let us down."

"I think that we have been looked after just like the Israelites were looked after when they wandered in the desert. God provided them with food and water," commented Katie Ann. "He provided us with a hen which instead of laying one egg a day has been laying six! One for each of us and one to spare! That has to be a miracle!"

"It was amazing that dad suddenly decided to ask Joel if he would carry two chickens on the plane!" Paul Junior added, "In a way that was a miracle, too! So was finding the river here and Luke writing out Psalm 121. It's all been amazing! It can't just be coincidences!"

"I guess loads of people have been praying for us, once they knew our plane was missing," Joel added. "God has been answering their prayers, too. Even our safe landing was a miracle. Suddenly, all the oil on the windscreen cleared for just long enough for me to see where I could make an emergency landing."

These thoughts made everybody really grateful to God and they thanked him together, then packed their belongings and started on the trail. For a while they followed the river, but when it began to twist and turn rather a lot, Joel thought they should take a more direct route through the forest. He was so thankful to have the compass because they could very well have ended up going round in circles. Their progress was still quite slow because although Katie Ann's ankle was improving, she still could not walk very quickly.

All the children had quite a lot to carry, too, which meant they got tired and needed to rest quite often. Luke was the youngest by far and he was being so brave—Paul Junior was so proud of his new buddy!

Joel began to think about what they would eat that day. Supplies from the tuck boxes were now almost completely finished. They needed something more substantial to keep them going. If they had kept following the river maybe they could have caught some fish. He began to doubt whether he had made the best decision.

Finally, he told the children to stop.

"Guys," he apologised, "I'm really sorry. I thought it was best to come through the forest, but I didn't pray about it first and now I'm not sure. I just thought that the river seemed to twist and turn so much, but now I realize that following it would mean we would still have a supply of clean water and maybe a fish, too. I think we should turn round and go back to where we left the river. I'm really sorry."

The children looked so tired and the thought of an extra hour's walking didn't thrill them with delight, but they knew that Joel was only doing what he thought was best for them all.

"Can we stay here and have a bit of a rest and a drink first?" asked Luke.

"Of course! Fifteen minutes time out before we set off again." He answered.

All their feelings of happiness had disappeared as the morning wore on. To make things worse it had begun to drizzle. They started to feel cold and the path became slippery.

"Let's sing as we go," suggested Katie Ann, "It always makes us feel better."

"We could sing that song from 'The Sound of Music', you know the one about 'my favourite things', replied Julienne, "Do you all know it? I just loved that film!"

Luke didn't know the song, but soon picked it up and singing helped them as they retraced their steps, not all the way to the waterfall but to where they had left off following the river.

"Hooray!" shouted Luke when he caught sight of the river again. They had wasted a couple of hours but Joel felt happier. He had learnt a lesson to pray about every decision.

The children's, as well as his life depended on it.

They trekked along the river bank for another hour and the drizzle stopped and the sun came out again. Once the rain stopped they noticed that snails were crawling everywhere so, they collected the largest they could find and put them in the empty cooking pot, carefully putting the lid on it to keep them from escaping. It wasn't easy to carry it upright, but the boys took it in turns. There were a lot of dark black volcanic rocks around.

"They are solidified lava from when the volcano erupted many years ago," explained Joel. "It's extinct now, but this lava rock remains."

At one place there were a lot of rocks and it seemed a good place to stop.

"I had thought we might have made it all the way down the mountain today, but I think we need to make camp again before it gets too late," explained Joel. It was the middle of the afternoon and they hadn't eaten since breakfast. Making a shelter and finding food and firewood would all take time. The sun would set soon after six because they were so near the equator.

Everyone spread their wet anoraks over the rocks to dry while they searched for things to eat. Paul Junior took his catapult with him. Maybe he would see a fat bird or something which they could cook with the snails. They all scavenged for wild celery and young bamboo shoots as well as anything which could be used as kindling for the fire.

How glad they were that Joel had carried the lining of the Cessna which he'd detached. At least they could sleep under a shelter.

They collected water from the river and as soon as they had a fire they cooked the snails. They also boiled more water for drinking. Luke made a kind of fishing line with some string, and a hook which he made from the pin of a badge he wore on his anorak. It wasn't very good, but he thought it might just work. He used to love to go fishing with his uncle when he lived in England.

"All I need is some bait," he told the others, "I need some worms or insects".

Soon he was provided with a cup with some insects in it. The rest of the group didn't think he had any chance of catching a fish, even if there were any in the river, but were happy for him to have a go. He was the youngest and had been very plucky all through the adventure. He must have been really scared at times.

While Luke was fishing, once the camp had been set up and the water was on the boil, the others went swimming. Joel was not only a good swimmer but he also had life-saving skills, so he joined them in the water. It wasn't a deep river, but the current was strong.

He had a sudden thought. If they could build a raft, they would soon get to safety! But how could they build a raft in this forest? Maybe they could hollow out a canoe? Then he realised that one would be too small for all of them.

His thoughts were interrupted by a yell from Luke.

Chapter thirteen

Everyone turned to look at Luke.

"I've got a bite!" he shouted, "It's fish for supper! I think it must be big, I'm having trouble pulling it up!"

Having said that, with a huge splash he slid off the rock and into the river. Luke could swim, but not that strongly. Trying to hold on to his fishing line and keep himself a float was almost impossible. Within seconds he was in difficulty. The river current was sweeping him downstream and all the water in his jeans was pulling him under.

In alarm Joel swam towards him. It took all his strength to hold Luke and swim back to the river bank against the current. Luke looked blue when he was finally dragged out of the river. Astonishingly, he had the string of the 'fishing line' wound so tightly around his wrist, that the fish which was well and truly hooked with the bent pin was hauled out of the water with him!

Joel had to turn Luke over on to his tummy and empty his lungs of the river water. Then he gave him some chest compressions and 'mouth to mouth' resuscitation until, thankfully, he was breathing normally again and his lips and cheeks had become pink. It could have been a fatal accident if Joel had not already been swimming in the river and was experienced in life saving! Poor Luke. At least he had the fish to show for all his trouble! He was very shaken and wet. The others all found him something to wear so, his wet clothes were spread out on the rocks to dry in the sun. Thank goodness the drizzle had stopped and it was warm again!

"I could do with a good cup of tea—English tea!" he said, "My mum says there's nothing like it for calming a person in a crisis!"

"The best we can do is to make some nettle tea," said Julienne at once. "Come on everybody, let's fill the cooking pan and please Joel, can you slash some nettles for us!"

"As soon as I'm dried and have my jeans on," agreed Joel. "I'm not letting those nettles touch my legs—I've never known such bad stingers!"

Everyone except Luke sprang into action. He was still trying to get warm and he was shaking all over. He looked at the now dead fish, lying beside him.

"What a lot of trouble you have caused," he told it. "I hope you are worth it!"

While the others were busy Luke realised how easily he could have died. He closed his eyes for a moment and talked to God.

"Thank you," he said, "You really did watch over my life."

Then he thought to himself. "What would have happened to me if I had died? Would I be in heaven with Jesus?" All his life he had been taught about how much God loved him, so much so that he had sent Jesus to earth to die in order that his wrongdoings might be forgiven and one day he could go to heaven for ever. He knew his parents had left England and gone to a remote part of the

Congo to tell the people there how much God loved them and if they asked for forgiveness for their sins they could be part of God's family. He knew that many of the people in the village where he lived had made that choice and become Christians. He had somehow thought that because his parents were missionaries then he automatically was a Christian, too. After the great shock of almost drowning, Luke knew that he wasn't yet a true Christian but he really wanted to belong to God's family and have Jesus as his Saviour and Friend. Sitting on the rock, still shaking, he quietly prayed a prayer.

"Father God, I am sorry for all the wrong things I have ever said or done. Please forgive me. Thank you for sending Jesus to die and take the punishment I deserve. I want to be your child in your family. Thank you for saving my life and giving me another chance to give my life to you. Help me always to follow you. Amen."

Luke opened his eyes. The sun was shining brightly and he felt warm and had stopped shaking. He felt sort of happy inside. He had meant the words he had said to God and knew that God had heard him and that he now belonged to the family of God forever. He knew too the Lord would always be with him and when he died, whenever that might happen, (and he hoped it wouldn't be for a long, long time), he would go to heaven.

Soon everyone was drinking hot nettle tea and eating a piece of crystallised pineapple from Katie Ann's tuck box. They knew that almost all the treats were finished, so they ate the piece very slowly, licking every last grain of sugar from their fingers.

"When I was in the river before Luke fell in," Joel told them, "I was wondering if we could make a raft or a canoe and get downstream that way. What happened to Luke taught me something—that it was not a good idea! It would be too dangerous! One small accident and someone could be drowned in this fast river. We shall have to continue on foot. Maybe tomorrow we will get down to civilisation."

"It taught me something, too," Luke told them all a little shyly, "Nearly drowning made me realise that I had never really become a Christian and I asked God to forgive me and be my Heavenly Father and Jesus to come into my life as my Saviour.

Joel put his arm around the boy's shoulder and beamed at him.

"Thank you for telling us that, Luke," he said, "That is the most wonderful and important decision that a person can make. That makes you my little brother!"

"Ours too," said Katie Ann and Paul Junior nodded in agreement.

"We both became Christians a little while ago. Welcome to the family!"

Julienne felt a little bit left out. She didn't understand what it really meant to 'become a Christian'. Since the plane crash she had begun to believe that God was real and what he said in the Bible was true, but there was so much she didn't know or understand. She decided she might ask Katie Ann to explain a bit more when they were walking together, trekking down the mountain.

"Thanks for the fish!" Julienne said to Luke. "Someone needs to take out the insides and backbone now, so we can cook it for supper."

Joel and Paul Junior took the fish to the riverside and cleaned it. It really was quite big and would be very tasty for their supper. They were hungry almost all the time now, but at least they were getting some food. Everything was served with boiled bamboo shoots, wild celery and nettles.

Julienne certainly did a good job with cooking the food they managed to scavenge. The others tried not to grumble even though they thought how wonderful it would be to have a hamburger and chips! They really tried to mean the words when they said 'grace' before they ate. God had provided for them and they were still alive!

The sunset that evening was brilliant! Once it was dark they settled under the shelter, huddling close together to keep warm and looking up at the stars in the sky. In a country where there are no lights at night the stars shine out really brightly and there are just so many of them to look at! Joel pointed out some constellations to the children and they dropped off to sleep thinking of the Great Bear and the Milky Way.

Paul Junior woke in the night when it was still dark. He lay still for a moment because he was sure he heard footsteps. Perhaps one of them had left the shelter to go to the latrine which Joel had dug for them in the trees. His eyes adjusted to the darkness and he counted the 'humps'. No, they were all there. What was he hearing? His heart began to beat faster and his mouth became dry. For some reason he felt very scared. He reached under his backpack which served as a pillow and felt for his torch. It was only to be used in emergencies, but somehow, Paul felt this was one. He had heard footsteps. He was sure it wasn't an animal. Maybe it was a rescuer looking for them, but why did he feel so scared? He turned on his torch and saw the barrel of a gun pointing at the group of bodies, behind which was a person in what looked like army uniform.

When the torch was switched on the man behind the gun began to shout in a strange language at Paul Junior. The rest of the Ace Survival Team woke at once. Whatever was happening?

Scared, the children tried to listen to what the man was saying. After all, you don't argue with a gun! Nobody could understand him.

"What do you want?" Joel asked in English. The man glowered and continued shouting.

Julienne spoke to him in French and Luke asked the same question in Kingwana, the language he spoke in Congo. The man still didn't understand them any more than they understood him.

For what seemed to be ages, they just looked at the man, who kept waving the gun around, pointing it first at one of them and then at another.

"He doesn't understand us," Joel said quietly to the children. "I guess he may be a poacher or a guerrilla soldier, but he seems alone. I want you all to pray, out loud and ask God to help and rescue us. The Psalm we keep reading tells us God never goes to sleep. Keep praying while I try to think of how to disarm him."

The children, now all very wide awake and sitting up began to pray out loud all at the same time. Scared as they were, they tried to make their voices work and reminded God of his promise to rescue them and watch over their lives and asked that he would help them right now!

Joel stood up so the man became agitated and walked up to him, pointing the gun almost into his chest. The scared children kept praying out loud over and over.

Then, from behind Julienne, Mrs Egg decided to join in and got out of her bag and began to cluck very loudly! The man swung round to find the chicken and in that moment, Joel grabbed his gun. The man pulled the trigger, but Joel had altered the angle of the gun so that when it fired it shot towards the ground. There was a terrible scream and the man fell to the ground.

Once Joel had disarmed him of the gun, he called out to Paul Junior,

"Bring the torch here, Paul."

The children had been frozen to the spot, but suddenly, Paul leaped into action and was by Joel's side with the torch. The man had shot himself in the leg. The wound was bleeding badly.

"Get me some water and the first aid box," he told the children. They got their torches and went to collect the First Aid box, also bringing some water to wash the man's wound.

"I've never had to do anything like this before. Please keep praying. The bullet must be lodged in his leg and I may have to try to remove it with my knife. I can't do that in the dark. For now, I'll just bandage it."

The man was now quiet and lying on the ground. The children were no longer scared of him. Katie Ann actually felt sorry for him. She remembered how much her ankle had hurt and still did a bit. She thought his pain must be far worse. She helped Joel by holding up his leg so that he could wind the bandage around it.

"Why don't we give him some pain killers and a drink of water?" She suggested and Joel agreed.

When he was bandaged they tried to make him more comfortable and lifted his wounded leg onto a boulder.

By this time it was getting light. Mrs Egg was once again being the wonder hen and laying eggs for them! Julienne was beginning to think she must be an angel in disguise.

As soon as it was really light, Joel and the children had to decide what to do. It was obvious the man would not be able to walk. They needed to strike camp and get down the mountain.

As usual they ate breakfast but also shared some with the man. Then, they made sure they all had enough water for the day ahead.

"We have to leave this poor man here," Joel told them, but I think we should leave the shelter over him. That way he will get shelter from the sun. As soon as we reach safety, we can send help for him."

"It's so hard to leave him. He won't die, will he?" asked Katie Ann.

"The bleeding hasn't come right through the bandages," said Joel, "so I think that he'll be alright. He can't walk and he's too heavy to carry. We'll give him another dose of pain killers and leave one bottle of water with him. Let's pray that we reach help quickly."

They packed up and were ready to start off. Joel had taken the gun for security reasons.

They started on the trek, having decided to stay close to the river. After they had gone a few yards, Katie Ann said to Joel,

"There's something I have to do first," and hobbled back with her stick to the shelter.

She bent over the soldier, put her hand on his forehead and prayed for him.

"We don't know who you are, but God does," she prayed, "May he bless you and heal your leg. Amen".

Chapter fourteen

What a day and night it had been! The group were all still tired when they set off. They were also a bit hungry as rations were now very meagre. Joel blazed a trail for them following the river, but not on the edge which was very muddy, but a little higher up where there was bamboo growing. This gave some shelter both from the sun and also the mist which always seemed to appear in the mornings.

They tried to sing as they walked along to help them forget the frightening night, but none of them had much energy or breath to do that. They were surprisingly quiet as they trekked, Joel first, followed by the girls and the boys at the back. So much had happened. Surely, their ordeal must be nearly over! Would they reach civilisation today? How much longer could they keep going? They knew that they had to be careful with water, having left one of the bottles with the night time intruder. Their spirits were very low.

After about an hour during which they had made good progress, Joel suggested they find a place to stop and rest for a short while. Katie Ann was very brave, but still hobbled along.

They came to what almost seemed like a clearing. Lots of the bamboo had been broken down and there were leaves scattered around. The children took off their backpacks and flopped to the ground, glad to rest. It seemed as if a depression had fallen over them all.

Joel kept wondering if they were going round and round in circles for he had expected, from his calculations, that they would have reached the lower slopes long before now. He was sure they must be on Mount Sabinyo, but if they were, then they should have made it through the forest before now. Had he got his calculations all wrong? Perhaps something was wrong with his compass.

Up in the sky another pilot was looking at his compass and checking his instruments. It was the chief helicopter pilot of the Rwandan military. He had been given permission to fly the private helicopter, belonging to the President of Rwanda, to help to find the missing children.

After George had located the crashed plane, he and Julienne's father had been trying to get help from the Congolese and Rwandan armies. It seemed that all the troops were engaged in exercises and they were almost despairing of finding any help. They had even put out an appeal on the Rwandan television news. The children had now been missing for several days. They might all be suffering from exposure up on the mountain. Maybe, they were injured too. The longer it was before they were found the less were their chances of survival.

The President had watched the appeal and responded at once. His private helicopter had been made available. George had been called out to collect a very sick patient and so was not available to accompany the pilot, but had given him all his data as to where they had located the missing plane. The pilot had taken with him two experienced soldiers and a game warden from the Virunga National Park, to help in the search.

The weather wasn't good. Once again, thunder storms were making flying treacherous, but the very experienced pilot managed eventually, to locate the plane. He hovered over the plateau where he decided to winch two of his three comrades down onto it as he didn't really have enough space to land safely. They were equipped with their 'walkie talkie' hand radios, which they hoped would work in the forest.

"Safely down," reported the soldier, as he sent the winch back for the park ranger, who soon joined him.

First, they inspected the plane.

"Broken piston," reported the soldier, "No sign of anyone here. They must all still be alive."

They then found the luggage with the notes attached and reported this to the pilot.

"Send everything up," the pilot requested, so all the bags were winched into the helicopter one by one.

"We will start trekking along the trail they will have cut," the warden said, "It should be easy to see where they have gone. We'll keep in contact. Over and out."

"Roger, message received," replied the pilot. "I will have to climb higher so will circle over the area. Try to keep in contact. I will return to the crash site at 15 .00 hours to pick you up unless you have contacted me to say otherwise. Over and out."

So the search began in earnest.

Meanwhile, down in the bamboo forest the children felt a bit better for a rest.

"Come on, Ace Survival Team," Joel encouraged them, "Let's see how far we can travel today."

They got up and put on their back packs and rather than have to cut their own trail, they found where the undergrowth had already been trampled down so that made it easier to walk, although Joel wasn't sure if they were on a regular trail or not and just hoped it would lead somewhere.

After about half an hour they were suddenly startled by a loud noise! They all turned round to look in the direction from where the noise seemed to be coming. Joel had raised the gun in case he needed it.

The noise came from a large creature, standing on its hind legs and banging its chest and making a roaring sound. It sounded angry!

To the children it looked like King Kong! It was so huge that they felt terrified!

Their first instinct was to take to their heels and run for their lives!

"Stop! Stay still!" said Julienne in a loud whisper. "Don't run! It's a gorilla. Put down the gun Joel and everyone crouch down. Don't stare at it but put your heads down."

Somehow, Julienne knew what they should be doing, so they all obeyed her.

"Keep very quiet and talk only in whispers," she said to them when they were all sitting on the forest floor.

"How do you know this?" whispered Katie Ann, who was next to her.

"Not long ago I saw a movie, 'Gorillas in the Mist'. Dad wants us to have a trip to visit the Gorillas, so the film was to tell us about them. I'm telling you what they said in that. That's a big silverback gorilla and he's defending his family."

After several minutes of the silverback banging his chest and showing his dominance, everyone's fear diminished a bit and it didn't seem as if their heart beats were banging in tune to the gorilla's chest banging! They glanced at him, but did not stare into his eyes. He was a magnificent creature!

After a while he was joined by a whole troupe of Gorillas, some large and some small, but none as big as he was and none of them had a silver back as he did. There was one mother with a tiny baby clinging to her chest. It was so cute and the children longed to touch it, but of course, they didn't dare to move.

There were several young Gorillas who were playful and romping around. They seemed to be pretend fighting just like children in a playground. Others in the troupe were pulling strips from the bamboo bushes and peeling them and eating them. They were devouring so many branches and so quickly! Now the children understood why the place where they had rested was so broken down, as was the trail they had followed from there. It must have been where the Gorillas had fed! Altogether they counted thirteen Gorillas in the family.

"How long do we stay here?" whispered Luke to Joel, for he was getting cramp in his legs?

"We stay like this until they have moved on," replied Joel. "We can't take any chances. If we anger or threaten that silverback, then he could chase us and look how big he is!"

"Yes, we just stay here until they have gone. They are supposed to be gentle creatures, but the dominant male will always defend his family," Julienne added. "I think they are vegetarians, so Mrs Egg should be safe." She cuddled the bag in which she carried the chicken. "We should just enjoy seeing the Gorillas, because my dad says it costs hundreds of dollars to come and visit them and we have got it for free!"

That is what they did, for maybe an hour. They were a bit cramped, the ground was damp and they had nothing to eat but they had an amazing view of these wonderful animals which very few people were privileged to see!

Sitting there quietly they were suddenly disturbed again by approaching footsteps. They all tensed up, not knowing what to do. Were there more guerrilla soldiers in the area or even poachers trying to capture these wonderful creatures? Pictures of the film she had seen flashed instantly through Julienne's mind where poachers had trapped Gorillas in order to cut off their hands which were sold illegally in some country which she couldn't remember, to be used as ash trays!

Instinctively, Joel put his hand out and reached for the gun. He had to protect the children! That was his first thought.

A hand grasped his shoulder. He turned around to see a park ranger and a soldier with him. The soldier had his hand on Joel's shoulder and wasn't going to let go in a hurry.

The ranger began to make 'gorilla like' noises to allay the fears of the silver back. It was almost as if he was talking to him. The Gorillas began to move further back into the bamboo forest.

The soldier whispered in a menacing voice to Joel, "So we have caught you! We knew a poacher had been setting traps! We didn't expect it to be a 'muzungu', (white man.) I see your gun, it is the type used by poachers. It is a very serious crime against these animals and the laws of our country! I arrest you now! You are also teaching the children this bad way of life!" he said, in his rather broken English.

Then he turned to the ranger and spoke in Kinyarwanda. At least Julienne thought it was that language because she caught a word or two which she had heard the housekeeper at home use.

Joel's hands were tied together and the gun confiscated in spite of his protests of innocence.

He tried to explain how he had acquired the gun and told them about the man who had disturbed them the previous night. The soldier didn't understand what Joel was trying to say even though he spoke as slowly as he could. His New Zealand accent didn't help, either.

Luke tried to talk to the game warden in Kingwana, the Congolese form of Swahili.

He wanted to tell him about the plane crash. Even though Luke had spoken that language fluently since he was old enough to talk, he was so scared now that his mouth was dry and the words wouldn't come easily. Julienne then began to explain in French, with the help of Katie Ann and Paul Junior, both of whom sometimes used French at home in C.A.R. Between the four of them they managed to make the ranger understand what had happened, but the soldier was unconvinced.

The ranger suddenly smiled. In French he told Julienne that yes, the rangers had been told to look out for people from a plane crash.

Attached to his uniform was a 'walkie-talkie' radio. He reached for it and began talking rapidly in Kinyarwanda.

"Yes, yes," he was telling his boss, "Yes we have found Gorilla Family 13, but yes, there is more. We have found a man and four children. They came from a plane."

He turned and talked to the soldier. "Yes it is true. Let this man go. Untie his hands. The President's men are searching for them. The helicopter is even now searching. We are heroes! We have found the missing children and the pilot! The President will be very pleased. Now we must treat our guests very well!"

The soldier, it has to be said, rather reluctantly untied Joel's wrists. He had hoped to be praised for catching the poacher but maybe he would be praised for finding the children, especially when the President heard who found them!

"Sorry, my friend Mr Pilot," said the soldier, in his broken English. Then he turned to the children, "Pardon, mes enfants, pardon-moi," he begged. He took off his back pack and rummaged around inside, finally pulling out a bunch of small bananas.

The children's eyes grew wide in anticipation. How sweet they looked! How hungry they all were! The soldier gave all the Ace Survival Team two each, leaving one for himself and one for the ranger.

They ate them in delight, saying 'thank you' in as many languages as they could muster between them. Seeing their delight the ranger also delved into his bag and produced some mangoes. What a treat! Joel cut them up with his knife and they all shared the delicious sweet, juicy fruit. It tasted the best food they had ever eaten!

The ranger was called up on his radio; yes, these were the missing children and their pilot. The President's men had found the plane and were even now trekking towards them but had a complication because they had found the wounded poacher.

"We are sending men with a stretcher to collect the wounded man," he was told on the radio. "A party of tourists are already on the mountain and will soon be in your area to view the Gorilla Family 13. Can you take the children down the shortest route to our visitor centre? The President's helicopter is coming in to land there and will take them to Kigali. Over and out."

"Roger," answered the ranger. "We will leave at once."

Chapter fifteen

In a mixture of French and English the ranger explained to them what was happening. He asked if Katie Ann could manage to walk down a steep track to the base of the mountain, because that was the quickest way to the visitor centre.

"I'm sure I can," she answered as Joel nodded and agreed that they would all help her.

Everyone's spirits were now high, having been so depressed earlier in the day! They began to sing as they started to walk down the track, the warden taking the lead and the soldier at the rear of the party.

Mostly, on their treks when they had sung, it had been ordinary songs which they all knew and liked, but this time, they wanted to praise God for their rescue. They began to sing hymns and choruses with great gusto.

"I sing, too," said the warden and the soldier also joined in with him.

Uwitteka n'umunyambabzi;
N'Umukunzi wac' udahemekuka;
Nta warondor imbarag'agira;
Nta wager' urukundo rwe rwinshi.

"We know that song, too!" shouted Katie Ann and Paul Junior, recognising the tune. "In English it is called 'How good is the God we adore'!"

They joined in and very quickly, Joel, Luke and Julienne had picked up the words, too.

They sang God's praises all the way down the mountain.

It was surprising how soon they arrived at the visitor centre. They were given such a welcome! Food and drink were produced and they were given hot water to wash in and had the luxury of using a proper toilet!

The President's helicopter was waiting for them, but before they climbed into it they were all presented with a certificate by the head warden.

"All our visitors who trek to see the Gorillas are given a certificate to prove they have braved the mountain and seen the treasures of the forest, the Gorillas. You, too, have done this, so I present you all with such a certificate, saying you have seen Family 13 of Gorillas. All I need are your names so that I can write them on the certificate. You will not forget your visit to Mount Sabinyo!"

"How could we ever forget this adventure?" Luke said, "I will never forget my first school run!"

They all laughed. It was good to be able to laugh now that they knew they were all safe and would soon see their parents again.

The adventure wasn't quite over. They still had the flight to Kigali in the Presidential helicopter. That was really exciting. Joel sat next to the pilot and was interested in all the controls. The children were happy to look out and see the countryside. The pilot flew low so that they were able to see the town of Muzanze and then they followed the road which wound through the hillside. Every now and then the pilot would point out a landmark to them. One was very sad. There was a little cemetery by the side of the road. It was a Chinese cemetery. Chinese labourers, some of them convicts, had been sent many years ago to build the road. They hadn't been used to the climate and lots of them caught diseases like malaria and died.

The pilot also pointed out to them a farm where cheese was made. Luke was amazed. There were black and white cows in a meadow, just like ones he would see in England.

"Wow!" said Julienne in surprise, "They are Dutch Friesian cows, not English!"

Rwanda was a surprising country!

Soon they reached the outskirts of the capital city, Kigali. They could see how it lay in a valley with steep hills around it. From looking out over small villages of little houses mostly with tin roofs, now they were over modern houses and even tower blocks. From the sky they could see the beautiful parks and the bushes planted between the carriageways. The rains had already started, so everything looked green and vibrant.

It seemed as if they crossed right over the city to reach the airport, called Kanombe Airport. The Pilot was speaking to the control tower.

"Yes, President One, the helipad is clear for you. No planes are moving in or out of the runway," the pilot was told. The helicopter landed in the special part designated for it. A large black car drove up to take the children and Joel over the tarmac to the terminal building. Their baggage was loaded into the boot and they were driven the few yards to the V.I.P. entrance. Five very unkempt people looked so different from the usual people who entered the terminal that way! Their clothes were dirty and torn and hair matted and tangled. Even so, people on the viewing balcony were waving and cheering.

"They must think we are important guests, or even that the President is with us!" giggled Julienne. "I always thought I wanted to be someone very important!"

They were ushered into the special lounge which the President used when he was flying from the airport. Inside their parents were waiting for them!

What a reunion it was! It had been the longest week that any of them could remember and there had been times when the parents wondered if they would ever see their children again and times when the Ace Survival Team wondered if they would reach civilisation. As if to echo what they felt Mrs Egg started to cluck away!

Joel had the biggest surprise of all. When his parents were informed that the plane he had been flying was missing, members of their community and church in New Zealand had clubbed together and bought tickets for them to go to Africa! He was overjoyed to see them again!

Once the great excitement had settled down, Julienne's father told them all that the Hotel Gorillas, had provided them all with rooms at the President's request.

"Even my wife and I are invited to stay there, so that we can all be together for a few days," he announced to them all. "The President has arranged for his chauffer to take us there and he will visit this evening to make sure that we are being well cared for. I am totally amazed at his concern and kindness!"

There were too many people to go in the one car, even though it was a very big limousine. Julienne's parents followed it taking their daughter, Katie Ann and her mom and small brother with them.

They were warmly welcomed at the hotel and shown to their rooms. There was just one small problem. Julienne was not allowed to take Mrs Egg into the bedroom! It was hard for her to part with her new pet. She begged the hotel manager to change his mind, but he was adamant. No chickens allowed in bedrooms! In the end her father promised to take Mrs Egg to their own home and ask their housekeeper to care for her until she eventually could be flown to Kenya. Julienne kept explaining that Mrs Egg was an extremely special hen, a sort of angel, who had produced an amazing amount of eggs every day and had helped them all survive.

Hot baths, hair washes and clean clothes made all the Ace Survival team feel wonderful! Even the boys appreciated being clean and tidy! They had to look good to greet the President.

After a wonderful dinner the group all gathered in the hotel lounge and the survivors told their story, bit by bit. Between them all and with the help of the journal they had kept, they were able to relate all their adventures, all the meals they had scavenged and cooked and all their prayers which had been answered. Even as they shared their story, the team were amazed again at how God had looked after them in every way from the moment the piston broke in the plane to the provision of hotel rooms in Hotel Gorillas.

The President of Rwanda arrived. He was tall and stately and the children felt shy and in awe of him, but he quickly put them all at ease. He spoke to them in flawless English and wanted them to repeat their survival story.

They told him everything, including the Psalm 121 which Luke had written out and said how much it had helped them.

"Yes'ashimwe!" exclaimed the President in his native tongue of Kinyarwanda. It meant, 'Praise God!'

When it was time for the President to leave, everyone present thanked him very much for his kindness.

"Would you be willing to do one thing for me?" he asked the Ace team.

"Of course," they replied.

"If I send reporters of the TV crew around, would you tell your story just as you have told me? I would like my people to hear how God has provided for you and looked after you and kept his promises to you. Please tell them about the miracle hen who laid so many eggs and don't forget to mention the beautiful Gorillas that did not attack you because you respected them."

Joel and the children promised to tell their story because they wanted others to know how wonderful God is to those who trust him.

After the President had gone everyone was still too excited to go to bed so they stayed up chatting together.

"Which part of the adventure was the most memorable for you?" Julienne's father asked his daughter.

"First of all, finding out that things like my new computer and my designer jeans are not really important, instead all of our lives are much, much more important. Then, learning that Jesus is alive, loves me and I could be his child. I know that I want to follow and love him all my life. Then, I learnt I could cook and loved being useful!"

Her father was very quiet.

"I think my daughter has learnt more than her father. Your mother started to pray and I was not pleased. I thought I was right in my belief that there is no God. I have to say, although I am not yet a believer, I now have an open mind. It really seems miraculous that you have all survived and I'm so grateful for that!"

"When I thought I could have drowned, it made me think, too," said Luke, "I gave my life to Jesus then. I wanted to know for sure that I was a child of God and would go to heaven when I die."

"Paul Junior and I," continued Katie Ann, "we have both learnt about believing what God says in the Bible is true and choosing to trust Him even when it was hard to do so."

Joel also had something to add.

"I want to say to your parents that they have the most fantastic kids. They didn't grumble and all worked together and shared everything. All through the adventure I knew the Lord was blessing us even though there were some very scary moments!"

Julienne looked at her parents.

"Please don't send me back to Holland to school. Let me stay at Hilltop High until it's time for university! After all we've shared together we are such good friends and we all need to help Luke settle in at school!"

Julienne's mother smiled. "I'm glad you want to stay there. I'm glad you have such good friends!"

"The school run will start again on Monday morning. You're booked on a Rwandair commercial flight from Kigali to Nairobi and the school bus will meet you at the airport. You'll have only missed one week of school." Paul and Katie's dad told them.

"Only a week! It seems like the longest, most exciting week of my life!" remarked Luke.

"And for all of us," added Joel. "We will always be, as Julienne nicknamed us, The Ace Survival team!"

Also available

THE CHOCOLATE CLUB

Mary Weeks Millard

Instead of being the saddest Christmas of her life, Rosanna's big idea transforms it into a wonderful time, not only for her own family but also for two disadvantaged families.The friendship between the children develops into a club—The Chocolate Club. They have fun and adventures together as they learn to pray and see miracles happen.

Mary Weeks Millard used to work as a missionary in Africa. She now loves to write stories for younger readers.

Also available

A COBWEB COVERED CONSPIRACY

Jill Silverthorne

Martin isn't in the 'in crowd'. School's hard work—particularly as he has to be friends with bully Joe Fuller. Then Martin begins to discover who his true friends are. Together, they begin to unravel a mystery more dangerous than they could ever have imagined. Pizzas, spiders and a dog called Becker all add to the plot, as Martin finds out about the one person who he can truly rely on.

Jill Silverthorne was born and bred in South Wales. She graduated from the University of Leicester with a degree in English and went on to pursue a career in teaching.

Also available

RICHES IN ROMANIA

Rebecca Parkinson

Jenny's parents have always been able to give her everything she wants until her dad begins a new job working for a Christian charity. As Jenny struggles to come to terms with their new lifestyle, her family is invited to take part in a farming project in Romania. As Jenny and her brother David spend time in a small Romanian village, they make friends with the local children and begin to realise that friendship can break down barriers of wealth, language and culture. However, when Jenny's precious locket goes missing it seems that everything has gone wrong, until a guard, previously in the Communist regime, teaches her the secret of forgiveness and encourages her to set about putting things right in her own life.

Rebecca Parkinson lives in Lancashire with her husband and their two children. As a teacher and the leader of the youth and children's team in her church, she loves to pass the Bible stories on to others in a way that everyone can understand.

Also available

THE SECRET OF THE HIDDEN TUNNEL

Mary Weeks Millard

Matty Morris's world collapses when her parents announce that they are going to move to Africa and that she will need to go to boarding school. She is sure she won't like St Anne's, but she quickly settles in and makes friends. Through a series of adventures and personal challenges she and her friends make exciting discoveries about the school's history as well as some life-changing decisions ...

Mary Weeks Millard used to work as a missionary in Africa. She now loves to write stories for younger readers.